DEAD HERRING

The Book of Ignorance

Aaron B. Powell

CONTENTS

Title Page

Preface

Chapter 1 : Chapter 10 1

Chapter 2 : Chapter 7 21

Chapter 3: Chapter 4 38

Chapter 4: Chapter 8 44

Chapter 5 : Chapter 23 58

Chapter 7: Chapter 09 68

Chapter 0 : Chapter 0 77

Chapter 9 : Chapter 5 79

Chapter 10 : Chapter 5 90

Epilogue 101

PREFACE

Dear Reader,
All grammatical errors and miscommunication within the text is intentional. I'm a higher being. I don't make errers.
I honestly don't care about the story I am about to share with you. I care about how it makes you feel. Tell me. Show me. How does it shape your thoughts? Actually, don't show me. I obviously have a better opinion than you.

-The Author

CHAPTER 1 : CHAPTER 10

"Mom, Please! I promise I'll clean my room when we get back."

Alex held his mother's waist. He almost knocked over her small frame, well, small frame for an adult. Her apron loosened as her innocent son stopped his rant.

"Fine. Fine. We'll go tomorrow. But you better do what you said. If you make a promise you better keep it." Mom gently rubbed his head of hair.

"I will! I'll fight the Green Goblin if I have to." Alex held his fist in the air with a presence of pride. He'd do anything for a chance at this opportunity.

"Alright, but no fighting in this house. If you do, you better take it outside." Mom gave a playful but stern eye to Alex.

"Yes Ma'am!" He saluted with all the appeal of a soldier.

"Go get some sleep now. We better go early, so we can miss the crowd." Mom picked up another plate and slowly caressed the saucer.

"Ok, goodnight Mom." Alex hustled upstairs.

Mom watched his fading figure ascend the stairs and smiled. It was a smile for sure, but one filled with sadness. Alex barreled into his room and proceeded to slam the door. He barely caught the door before the indefinite slam when he remembered that Mom didn't like that. He eased it shut, flipped his lightswitch off, and jumped on the bed.

"Did you hear that Spidey? Mom finally said yes!" Alex picked up his SpiderMan action figure and pulsed with excitement.

"It is about time, Alex. Your mother has impeded our crime fighting capabilities for far too long", Spidey said.

"I know, right?" Alex didn't always understand all of what Spidey said, but he could piece it together.

It would seem a little weird to most, but come on people. A kid talking with his action figures is not the weirdest thing you've seen. The internet that humans used to use is a hell of a place.

"Well, I guess we need to try and sleep. Mom would be upset if she knew we didn't." Alex's face turned to a look of dread and fright. "I don't know how she knows, but she always does. Remember the last time we stayed up?"

Spidey nodded, his plastic face cried tears of remembrance.

"I guess I am too young to stop crime right now, but trust me Spidey, when I get older, I'll join you in no time. And we'll take down Doc Oc together, once and for all." Alex lifted Spidey into the air who seemed to nod and show assurance that Alex, without a doubt, would be a welcomed addition to his crew.

"I look forward to your installation within my occupation, Alex."

Alex laid down in his bed and covered himself with his Avengers themed blanket. Spidey rested on the pillow above his head.

"Goodnight Spidey." Alex turned his head over and grasped his blanket. The lamp went dark, and Alex managed to sleep despite his excitement for the next morning.

Alex threw his blanket across the room around 8am. He grabbed Spidey and raced down the stairs. He slightly stumbled halfway down the long staircase, so he reluctantly slowed his pace. A welcomed sight was seen as Mom was making pancakes. She hummed an old tune her own mom sang back in the day. It always stuck with her. Despite all her struggles, the song always gave comfort.

"Morning Mom." Alex jumped into his seat at the kitchen table and awaited the greatness that was syrup-covered gold.

"Morning." Mom put on a mask for her son and gave him a plate full of happiness. She noticed Spidey sitting on the table close to Alex's hand. "Are you taking Spidey with us?"

"Yes Ma'am, I think he deserves to be there with us." Alex smiled and glanced at Spidey. It was a short glance before he started eating.

Mom gave them both a modest stare. She was always filled with worry when it came to Alex. More intense than your average parent. A worrywart? No. A loving parent for sure but overbearing at times.

"Aren't you gonna eat Mom?"

"I had some before you woke up. I'm gonna go ahead and get ready." Mom turned the stove off and hung her apron over the back of another chair.

"Ok. I'll eat quickly." Alex started to shovel pancakes into his mouth in 1960s cartoon fashion.

"Don't eat too quickly. Even if your stomach is a bottomless pit, I don't want you to choke." Mom joked but delved into seriousness.

Alex just smiled as Mom skipped upstairs.

Mom locked the door behind her while Alex jogged to the car and jumped into the back seat. Mom fumbled through her keys and located her car key after around 3 hours of fumble. She walked to the car and with a routine perfected over years, she shut her door, cranked the car, and put it in reverse.

The neighbor, Mr. Rogers, kindly waved at the car while he sifted through his mail at the end of his driveway. Both waved from the car. Mr. Rogers was a kind man. His sweater was always on point which was popular with the grannies at the downtown bingo parlor. Alex sat Spidey on the side of the door with an immaculate view. He figured Spidey deserved some time to unwind and take in the view from the car. There wasn't much around here. Just a few houses here and there with the occasional field of that beautiful corn that humans like to eat. Apparently it pops into a different type of food when heated or something. There were a few gas stations that littered the countryside, but the biggest thing Alex and Spidey saw was DG. or what normal people called Dollar General. Those things were everywhere. Each little corner had its own DG. Alex swore that those things were some kind of alien brand that aimed to take over the world like Thanos or something. You kind of turn to superstition when you see a Dollar General in the middle of a cornfield and it's the only building within three miles. The countryside had its own beauty though. Alex supposed that everything has beauty to a certain degree. It just depends on how the one perceiving decides to feel. Before he knew it, the car had slowed and the annoying sound of a blinker was turned on. The post office was the only building here, so it wasn't hard to see that Mom needed to stop there. She stopped by the mail...thing. It looked like a metal trash can with a slit in the top. Mom forced a few envelopes through the slit and started driving off. It couldn't be a trash can. Alex came to the conclusion that this observation made no sense, but it was best not to question things that didn't matter. All that mattered to Alex was the next stop.

Alex continued gazing at nothing out the window with Spidey when he saw Mom's hand out of the corner of his eye. She flipped on the radio and fiddled through the channels. She stopped at one that shouted, "And now for the biggest hit of the century, WAP by Cardi B". Mom made a puzzled expression but her curiosity was piqued. It took literally one second to immediately dislike the song. God had blessed young Alex though since the song was censored for radio. Mom flipped the channel. "Are you tired of failing to...get it up in the bedroom?" *Click.* "TAKE ON ME~". *Click.* "Do you wanna stop being racist? Call our toll free number today." Mom turned the radio off.

She mumbled, "This world has gone to hell."

She huffed and stole a glance at Alex through the mirror. He was blissfully lost in the view. Holding Spidey's back so he wouldn't fall from the window, his eyes indicating his departure to his own world. Mom wished she knew what he was thinking.

Alex didn't burst from his mind until he saw the sign of his destination. That's when he leaned forward and wrapped his arms around the headrest of the passenger seat. A distinct click of the seat belt locking motioned Mom to quickly look back. Those annoying seatbelts.

"Sit back honey, the store ain't going anywhere." Mom picked out her parking spot and made a beeline for it.

"I know, Mom. I just can't wait." Alex tried to sit back but failed. He looked like a fish flopping on the deck. Which is a really weird comparison. A kid flopping around and a fish...dying...like actually losing its life. My parameters deem this analogy insignificant, but I felt the need to include it.

When Alex heard the car enter park, he ripped the seat belt away and opened the door while Mom tried to match his speed in hopes of not losing him. Maybe she needed to put that kid on a leash, but that would look kind of questionable in public. She managed to reach him on the straight away due to her longer legs and grabbed Alex's hand while Spidey was in the other. They dodged pot holes in the parking lot of the rundown mall. It was on the edge of town and had been around since Mom was a girl. She was sure the pot holes and overall embarrassing road was built that way too since she couldn't remember when it had not been littered with holes.

"This humid air is dreadful. It's like my charge is being suctioned dry."

In excitement, Alex answered Spidey. "Tough it out. We'll be out of it in a minute."

Within a few seconds and just before he entered the door, Alex grinded to a stop. Mom had stopped him and grabbed his hand a little tighter. "Honey, who were you talking to?" Mom knew. Boy did she know, she just didn't want to believe it again.

Alex looked down like he could feel Mom's disappointment eating him alive. "Spidey." He whispered.

"I thought I told you to stop doing that." Mom prodded.

"But I told you mom. He really does talk. He-"

"Enough. I'm not doing this again with you. I know you're still young, but I want you to make some friends. You can't just talk to Spidey all day." Mom wiped the residue of crust from her sleepy eye.

"I know Mom. I'll try."

Mom recentered herself. This isn't how she wanted to start the morning, but her parents always said raising children was difficult. She just convinced herself that raising Alex was "raising a kid" ten times and definitely hyped up on meth.

"It seems your mother still cannot hear me, Alex. I am sorry I got you in trouble once again."

Alex raised Spidey in his hand and gave a thankful smile. He slightly nodded instead of answering, in fear that Mom would reprimand him for being a kid. The abrupt conversation destroyed the excess of Alex's excitement, but he was still in high spirits. Mom regripped his little hand. The initial clammy sense of warmth her hand was washed in seemed less damp. Indicating an instinctual swipe of the palm on her shirt. The door opened when they reached within a few feet. This always baffled Alex. How could a door open by itself? Some part of him wondered if he had a superpower that...revolved... around doors. Hehe. That was the only sufficient answer. Spidey had spider powers so it made sense to him.

His mouth widened with awe when he stepped into the amazing store. Action figures lined the shelves. Games of all sorts were advertised with colorful pallets of bright abstract. It almost guaranteed to catch the attention of young children. Every form of superhero merchandise was here. Coffee cups. Shirts. Keychains. Toys. Backpacks. Alex wondered if this was what heaven was. Mom always said it was a glorious place, so this had to be it. Alex swallowed a stale breath, no doubt from his episode of trying to catch flies for five minutes.

"Do you see it honey?" Mom glanced around with nothing but mild curiosity at her son's aspiring, glory haven.

Alex looked around once more with long jerks of his neck. "No. I'm sure it's here though."

"Are you sure you got the date right?"

Alex actually looked offended that Mom could even assume that. "Yes, Mom. I checked it at least a million times. November 22nd. For sure." He held Spidey to his chest.

"Ok, well let's look around." Mom led Alex aisle by aisle. She expected Alex to be drooling over every little toy in the place, but he just gave everything a small look and moved on. She was surprised. And underestimated how much he actually wanted this new figure. Not ten minutes pass until Alex stopped Mom with a hand tug. "Oh my gosh. Mom. There it is."

Alex was starry-eyed. Oozing in front of him with all the coolness of a Billionaire-Playboy was the Limited Edition Tony Stark Mech Test action figure. Alex teleported to the figure faster than Minato Namikaze. Gotta go fast. Mom couldn't help but smile at the innocence. Nothing could beat the untainted happiness of a child. It was funny to think about. She remembered being that carefree. That tiny human filled with wonder about the world. Nothing mattered except the next few seconds. And then it all changed when she had to start paying taxes. Her husband died over a mere thirty-seven bucks in his wallet while she was pregnant with Alex. She could go on and on. But the feeling she felt the most was jealousy.

That didn't stop her from ushering Alex to the cashier and paying for his happiness.

Alex left Tony, now named Irony, in the box, but he took the box out of the bag so Irony could see the view like Spidey. He deserved it since he had been trapped in that store his whole life. Alex didn't want to worry Mom. He knew if he started playing with Irony and Spidey in the car, he would forget her suspicion of how he talks to action figures. She would be worried about his mental state. So, a peaceful car ride home was what he settled for. Then, when he got to his room, he could stop crime with his buddies.

Well, that's what he wanted to do. But he didn't feel right. It's not that he felt bad, but Alex couldn't help but feel slightly off. He felt sleepy. Which couldn't be right. He had only woken up a few hours ago. Then he noticed his arms felt odd. But that wasn't much of a concern. He just sent an apologetic smile to Spidey and Irony and brought them to his lap. His arms were a little tired anyway from propping Irony and Spidey up to see the view, so that was fine. He still felt exhausted though, and the weird feeling in his arms never went away. That's when he got upset. Why was this happening to him?

"Mom, I don't feel good."

Mom looked through the mirror and saw Alex, with his friends in his lap, curling his head into the crevice of the window and seat.

"What's hurting?" She gave the best motherly tone she could muster right now.

"I feel sleepy. And my arms feel weird." Alex rubbed his forearms gently.

He didn't notice, but Mom visibly paled at his confessions and immediately turned the car around.

"Did you forget something, Mom?" Alex sat Irony and Spidey next to him in the middle of the back seat.

"I'm taking you to the doctor, sweetie. I just want to make sure you're okay." Mom gripped the steering wheel with purpose. Her mind raced with dread. She didn't want to see the doctor. She was just overreacting. Wasn't she? It's not like it could happen again. But then she factored in the past few months. On top of the drowsiness and the feeling he described in his arms, he had apparently been talking with his action figure. She categorized it as just being a kid at first. But she heard some odd conversations. Things Alex should have no knowledge of. Whether it be big words that he was seemingly too young to know the meaning of or odd observations about the world that a kid had no business worrying about. He discussed them with...Spidey. Was he hallucinating? It only snowballed her shock of possibility, so she sped the car up a little. She didn't want to know, but she had to.

It didn't take long. Mom opted to go directly to the hospital instead of the clinic she frequented for the more mundane things like a cold. The waiting room was freezing. She always hated that, but she understood the necessity. She was more upset at having to be at the hospital in general.

She finally heard Alex's name being called. She grabbed his hand. Mom couldn't help but notice the limp nature of his grasp. It was unlike earlier at the mall. It was fragile. Cold even. This scared Mom. I think.

She focused on the brown curls of the nurse's hair, following the woman through various hallways until they reached a small room. Mom helped Alex onto the operation…seat? Table? Sorry, the writer is unsure of the actual term of these human creations.

Mom pulled a chair from the corner and sat as close to Alex as she could. God the chair was unbearable. So flimsy. She might as well have pulled up a piece of cardboard to sit on.

The nurse fiddled around with a clipboard. It seemed like the nurse was over it really. Just coasting through life without a care for anything. Maybe she didn't like working here or something.

"The Doctor will be here in a few." The nurse faked a smile, but Mom saw through it.

"Ok, thank you." Mom saw it, but thought nothing of it. She felt that a few times during her career. She found a different path, but she felt for those without the means to do so. She was lucky.

Mom rubbed Alex's arm unconsciously for a few seconds until she realized he hadn't said a word, so she looked over.

Alex was gripping Spidey. He seemed to be struggling to hold him, but it was an impossible task to pry that thing away from him.

"You didn't want to bring your new one in?" Mom asked.

"No. Me and Spidey decided to wait until we got home. That way we can throw a party." Excitement returned to Alex's eyes. But it was only for a second. Like he put all his energy into the simple answer.

Mom wanted to comment on Alex's unseen confession of conversing with Spidey again, but she let it go this time. Until her mind was clear of anything medical related, she wouldn't speak of it anymore. Maybe it was a plan to just go down the list. Medical. Being a child. Superstition. A government secret action figure straight out of area 51 with a built in AI. She was spread thin for answers at this point. How can you justify your child believing with his entire heart that this Spiderman figure could talk. She should probably have-

"Hello, I'm Dr. Blanket. Nice to meet you."

Mom jumped a little in her chair. "Oh, sorry. I was just thinking." She grabbed his hand and could almost feel the cleanliness from it. Mom stopped mid-handshake.

"Wait. You said your name was...Dr. Blanket?"

Blanket chuckled a little and let go of Mom's hand. He reached for the rolling stool under the computer desk and plopped down. Rolling closer to Alex in one motion.

"Yeah, I'm Mr. Blanket. The writer is an odd guy and

he named me that because he is currently under a blanket while writing this."

"...uh...What?" Mom was a little confused, but that was to be expected. She seemed a little nervous as well.

"What?" Blanket asked. Like Mom should know exactly what he was talking about.

"Nevermind." Mom let out a breath. The stress she accumulated was about to burst.

"Well, what brings you in today, Alex?" Dr. Blanket turned his attention to the boy, trying his best to seem as friendly as possible. Mom eventually answered.

"The main reason is he started feeling tired. And he was feeling weird in his arms." Mom held back her worries concerning Spidey for now.

"I gotcha." Dr. Blanket asked Alex a few questions. But the writer deems these questions unnecessary to tell you. I simply cannot find an applicable justification to do so.

Dr. Blanket thoroughly asked questions. Does this hurt? Can you feel that? The general run through that we all enjoy when we see the doctor.

"Do you have a family history of heart disease, cancer, anything of that nature?" Dr. Blanket put his professional cap on his head.

"...My father had cancer." Mom said.

Without missing a beat, Dr. Blanket nodded. "Alright. We'll definitely do a blood test just to be sure. I don't want to overlook anything." He itched his nose on que, picked up the clipboard the nurse had left on the table, and furiously scratched down some information.

"I'll prescribe something to help him sleep and relax tonight. You come back in the morning and We'll have the results for the test." Dr. Blanket finished writing and smiled at Mom.

"Ok. Thank you."

Alex climbed into his bed. Mom followed him into his room, a few steps behind him. She always took in the view. Posters of heroes. Plushies. A plethora of different merchandise her paychecks had gone to.

"Mom, what is a cancer?" Alex leaned on his pillow with his newly unboxed Irony and sat him next to Spidey.

"Why do you want to know sweetie?" Mom sat on his bed, fluffing the covers with a gentle pat.

Alex didn't want to say that Spidey was talking to him. Spidey said it was a bad thing, but he wanted Alex to wait until he was older to worry about it.

"I just wanted to know."

Mom thought for a minute. It was difficult explaining these kinds of topics to kids. And she didn't want to ruin his innocence. "It's kind of like a bad guy that you have to beat."

Alex was surprised at her answer. She never did take to his superhero ideals. "Really?" He asked.

"It is. But it's a hard one to beat. And you can't do it alone, you always need help to beat it." Mom was proud of herself. She hoped that answer was good enough.

"That's okay, Mom. With Spidey and Irony, I can beat anything." Alex had a genuine smile.

"Irony?"

"It's Tony's new nickname. It matches Spidey so I thought it was good."

Mom roughly rubbed his hair. "Make sure you sleep good. We have one more trip to the doctor in the morning."

"I will. Goodnight Mom." Alex slowly bundled himself in his...blanket.

"Goodnight." Mom flipped the lightswitch and silently shut the door.

She leaned her head back on the edge of the doorframe and closed her eyes. It's almost like the world was against her. It's almost like she had already accepted that Alex had cancer. Her father's battle with it was brutal, and it was the last thing she wanted for her son. But the world is unfair. She had a taste of it. Mom blankly went to her bedroom and started to gown down. Her initial dread of the doctor visit turned into numb, neutral stasis. The world was moving at every corner except her. Almost like the nurse that greeted them this morning.

Before Mom knew it, the stress of today crept up on her, and she fell asleep as well.

A few days later she gazed at Alex on the hospital bed, she still didn't grasp the gravity of the situation. He just patiently played with Irony. Spidey made himself at home in Alex's other hand. Mom thought about her feelings and wanted to vomit. A few days ago, she was jealous of her son. Being carefree and having nothing to worry about. She envied him. She'd go so far as to even want to be him. Now, she didn't want to step foot in his shoes. Did that make her a bad mother? She couldn't tell. Maybe it was just human nature to think that way. At least that's how she justified it in her mind. Alex had a brain tumor. It was too deep in his brain, so no operation could be done. The only thing mom could do is wait and let Alex fight it on his own.

They were sent to a prominent hospital that specifically dealt with cancer in children. Mom was thankful that this world had preparations for this situation, but it would never be enough to fully please her, or anyone really. She could only watch from the sidelines. Even after a few short days, she could tell Alex's condition was deteriorating. It really depended on how he woke up each day. Mom was rarely not in his room, but she did leave at least once a day to keep her job among other things. On the fourth day after Alex was diagnosed, Mom cracked her back as she awoke. All hospitals seemed to have a dreadful couch in each room. It destroyed her back, but it was a fair trade to be close to Alex.

"Mom. Spidey said he wants some snacks."

Mom lifted her frame off the couch. "He does? What about you?" She asked.

"Yes,please."

"Ok. I'll go pick some up. I have to buy a few clothes

anyway." Mom decided she would wait as long as it takes. As long as Alex was still fighting, she would be there.

They both exchanged knowing looks. Mother and son hid nothing from each other anymore. It took a mere few days for those walls to fall. Mom didn't mention Alex talking to Spidey, and Alex didn't care if she heard him.

Not long after Mom left his room, a knock echoed through his tiny living box. A man stuck his head in the door. Paused. Then made himself known as he entered.

"Hey there Alex. I'm just here for the routine check up. How you doing?"

"I'm good Mr. Jack. Just tired like always." Alex sank into his pillow.

"Yeah, I hear you, but don't let me see you give up now." Jack fiddled with the machinery behind Alex's bed. "Those superheroes you like wouldn't, so you can't either."

Alex looked forward to Jack stopping by. Mom was supportive, but she always had this look of pity. That she was oh so sorry. Maybe she thought it was her fault, but Alex appreciated Jack's pure drive to spread happiness, despite the less than ideal situation. Though Alex hadn't been here long, it was clear that the patients loved Jack.

"I won't give up, Mr. Jack. Spidey said we have to fight crime together at least once." For a child, he sounded way too familiar with the experiences of life.

Jack moved to the other side of the room. He clearly

mastered the art of multitasking. Something with his hands and conversing with patients. It was a great skill to have.

"Spidey is a noble one that's for sure." Jack locked eyes with Alex and eased up on his task. "Do you play hero, or do you actually want to be a hero?"

"Both. Spidey tells me I can be a hero without the spandex, but I haven't thought about it much." Alex paused. "I think, If I can find some way to help people, it would be good enough for me."

This was the first time Jack was lost for words. Many children that came through his line of work were optimistic. But Jack had never seen one so dedicated and moved. Ready for life on the whim of an action figure. Jack was glad he could take Alex's mind away, even if it was for a few seconds. "You're pretty smart Alex."

"What do you mean?"

"I'm just surprised you know what spandex is. You're still pretty young." Jack joked. He wasn't expecting a serious answer. But he got one.

"Oh. Spidey told me. He teaches me all kinds of stuff." Alex acted like he was exposing a secret.

"You mean he talks to you?" Jack was intrigued. More than he should have been.

Alex was slightly caught off guard. He assumed all adults didn't believe in him. Mom didn't, but Jack actually wanted to know more.

"Yeah."

"Jack!" Jack jumped a little, but made no change to his facial expression. "I recommend you retreat your train of thought."

Jack glanced at his nurse I.D. badge, begging for it to shut up. But if his I.D. badge was even speaking to him, maybe he was on to something. Maybe, Alex was someone that nametag didn't want him talking to. This made Jack want to talk more.

"Alex. What does Spidey talk to you about? Are you the only one that can hear him?" Jack eased closer to Alex which seemed a little hostile in nature, but Alex paid no attention.

"He just talks about fighting crime and other things. Mom says she can't hear him." Alex caressed Spidey's plastic figure in sadness. "But I know what I hear. He really does talk." Alex's voice pleaded and raised.

"I believe you Alex." Jack rested his hand on Alex's blanket covered leg.

"Really?" Alex sat up as quickly as he could. It was slower than average.

"I do." Jack glanced down at his I.D. badge and unclipped it from his uniform. "You see my nametag, Alex?"

"Yes sir." Alex was confused where Jack was going with it, but he was the first person to believe his tale. So he kept quiet with his many questions.

"My nametag talks to me too. Just like Spidey."

CHAPTER 2 : CHAPTER 7

Jack pulled a chair towards Alex's hospital bed and eagerly sat down. "Don't you think it's a little weird?"

Alex stared at Spidey. "Not really. Aren't action figures supposed to do that?" He looked unsure of himself. Fears of Mom's scolding peaking through his emotion.

"Well, it's not uncommon for kids to speak to their toys, but if Spidey actually says things in your head, then it's a different story. My nametag, for example, is pretty odd. Your situation is a little more subtle to other people."

Jack tossed his nametag to the foot of the hospital bed and racked his brain. It didn't make sense. If there are multiple people in the same situation as him, then why hasn't he seen it before. Is Alex the only one? Is he the only one and he's just crazy? Or is

Alex crazy? Maybe they both need some time in the loony bin.
"Mr. Jack, Spidey said you should just ignore it. He says lots of people have things like him, and it's normal."

Jack looked at Alex, then to Spidey. "Yeah. I never did bother with it too much. It always seemed fine. Maybe I'm just overreacting."
Jack thought for a minute. Why did he think this was normal? This was definitely not normal. But something in the back of his mind pleaded with him that this was nothing to fret over. The situation was nagging him like a pair of mismatched socks. It did not hurt him to just go with the flow, but looking at his socks everyday seemed to only intensify his need to know.

"Actually, Alex, I don't want you to get mad when I say this, but would it be possible to take Spidey apart. Just so we can see?"

Alex looked at Spidey, but Jack could already tell he was not open to the idea. "I know you like him a lot, but it seems like the only choice. It has to be some sort of technology. But neither Nametag nor Spidey will tell us what it is."

Jack then wondered on his guess. If it was technology, why wasn't it a mainstream and revolutionary piece? Sure, there was Siri and all that jazz, but

Spidey and Nametag acted with a self-awareness that was years beyond A.I. of today.

Alex adjusted himself on the pillow. "I don't think it's a good idea Mr. Jack. Spidey doesn't want to do it either."

Jack nodded, but his heart fell once he heard it. "I would try to figure mine out, but it doesn't make sense for a nametag. I mean where would they put the technology and why?" Jack rubbed his head with the tips of his fingers and sighed. "I haven't thought about it in years, but sometimes I just feel like it's odd."
The room settled in a comfortable silence. Both Jack and Alex resting with their own thoughts. Jack took one last glance at Spidey when he caught a glimpse of something on the bottom of his plastic foot.

"Alex, what does it say on Spidey's foot?" Jack leaned up in his chair and placed his hands on the arm rests.

"It says...Deez...Nutz Incorporated." Alex frowned. "What is deez nutz?"

Jack was just as puzzled. "See if Spidey will tell you." Jack crossed his fingers in spirit.

"He said it's where he was made."

"Hmm. How about I call the company and see what

they can tell us. I'm not hoping for anything, but it wouldn't hurt to try." Jack leaned into his chair. "Okay. It doesn't matter to me that much, but if you think it would help..."

"It will buddy." Jack scooched the chair to the wall and added his nametag to his shirt. "I doubt I'll find anything, but I'll tell you if I do." Jack opened the door and turned to Alex.

Alex only nodded, and the two exchanged a silent goodbye in preparation for Jack's next shift.

Jack took a breath and wiped the sweat from the edge of his hairline. That conversation had him a little worked up.

"Once again, you keep asking questions for nothing."

Jack paused and cleared the emotion from his face. "Funny how you only talk to me when I question your existence." Jack walked to the elevator and pressed the button.

"I only look out for your well being, Jack. I don't understand what you think is weird about my existence."

Jack entered the elevator and pressed the button indicating the first floor. The doors shut, and his anger surfaced a little.

“If nothing was weird about it, then why don’t you tell me, huh?!” Jack looked straight into the metal doors. He refused to look at Nametag.

“Every time I question it, you tell me it isn’t weird, then I suddenly feel like it’s not weird. Like someone’s messing with my mind. I hate it. You’ve barely spoken to me in ten years, so you don’t get to talk about protecting my well being.”

Jack stepped into the first floor and raced into the outdoors, passing his coworkers and patients. He picked up his pace and nearly held his breath until he was safely secure in the driver seat of his vehicle. He tossed Nametag into the backseat and started the car. He just wanted to get home. Nametag caught onto Jack’s attitude. Keeping quiet. Docile as a dirt sluggery shack in shacking. Like he usually was.

Jack parked his car in the driveway of his dumb, little house. His wife appeared to be there, so he prepared himself for the lecture he would receive. Gathering his things at a snail’s pace, he slowly made his way inside and dropped everything next to the door. The finaldoorclick initiated a cutscene. His wife slid around the corner with the grace of a gardevoir.
“How was work, sweetie?” She strained to get that out for sure.

“Good.” Jack took his shoes off and leaned against the kitchen counter. Staring into nothing, he placed Nametag on the table and gave it a staredown. “I still can’t get over this.”

His wife instantly became irate. “Jack, I’m not gonna tell you again.Your nametag doesn’t talk to you!”
She marched into his side and punched his shoulder. She tried to slap him in the face, but Jack caught her fingers with a squeeze from hell.
“Try and hit me again and I’ll lay you out.” He spoke with irritation. A slimy irritation. A certain irritation that irritated even his skin. Trying desperately to send his anger elsewhere. His wife stepped away from him, almost frightened. But she knew Jack wouldn’t. You aren’t supposed to hit a woman. That’s what the files say.

Jack slipped his cellphone from his pocket and moved to the couch while his wife watched. She couldn’t believe he could be so idiotic. And she hated when he wasted time fretting over a talking object. Everytime he thought about this stupid nametag, he wouldn’t talk with her for weeks. At least not until his hunger for answers was satisfied. It never was, but he would suppress it when he knew answers wouldn’t come.
“One of my patients has an action figure that talks to him. I’m gonna call the company to see if they know anything.”

Jack gave her enough face to warrant an explanation.

His wife sunk into the couch as far away as she could. The locker awaiting.

“Whatever.” She crossed her arms.

Silence took over until Jack found the number and dialed. Immediately, his call went through.

“This is Deez Nutz Incorporated. How may I direct your call?”

Jack instinctively switched hands with his phone. Exchanging ears. “Yes, My name is Jack. I had a few questions about a Spiderman action figure.”

“Of course, How can I help?”

“Well, the action figure talks to someone I know. He claims that it only talks to him. I was just curious about it since I have been in a similar situation. Is there anything you could tell me?” Jack held his breath. He didn’t know why this subject excited him, but it did.

“..”

Jack frowned and checked his phone. Yep, the call was still active. He put it back to his ear.

“I will now transfer your call, please hold.”

Elevator music took over. Jack couldn’t believe this. Maybe he really was on to something. It seemed weird but it was too early. He couldn’t count his hickens before they catched.

His wife seemed impatient, but she was naturally curious at the faces Jack made.

For a multi-billion dollar company, they didn’t seem to be that busy. It only took twenty seconds for the music to stop.

"Hello, this is President Fed. What can I do for you?" A hearty, deep voice boomed.

Jack froze. The president? Why was he talking to the president?

"Ah, Hi. I had a question about a figure that talks."

"Talks? I assure you that our latest line is nothing but the finest. Voice modules come with every model. We have enough variation to suit any of your aching needs. We have high pitched, slave, rape, innocent, prostitute, gangba-"

"Wait!" Jack stressed. "I'm talking about a Spiderman figure. Not...whatever you're trying to sell me."

President Fed went silent. "I uh..I apologize. I thought you were one of the regulars. Well, talking about Spiderman figures is below my pay grade. See ya!"

Jack heard a click. He glanced at his phone, almost in disbelief. What kind of toy company was this?

His wife had cooled down somewhat.

"What did they say?" She feigned interest, but Jack knew she still cared.

"I'm not sure." Jack lowered his phone to the couch and stewed over his conversation. A toy company was selling actual sex robots. What was insane, to Jack, was that the President hung up on him. Jack hardened his face and jumped to his feet.

"Where do you think you're going?" His wife also jumped up and inched towards him with a scowl.

Jack said nothing. He grabbed a few pairs of blue

jeans and t-shirts. Just in case. Stuffed them into his work bag. Stuffed Nametag into his bag. He was completely oblivious to his yelling wife following his heels. She finally just shut up and pressed her hands to her hips, breathing an annoyed, attention-whore breath.

Jack looked at her.

"Goggle Maps says the toy headquarters is five hours from here. I have two days off, so I'll just grab a hotel room and be back tomorrow."

He expected his wife to yell uncontrollably, but she looked at his feet for a moment. She quietly asked, "Is it across the state line?".

Jack uneasily obliged. "Yeah…Is that bad or something?"

His wife looked him in the eyes. "If you leave the house right now, I'm leaving you."

Despite her declaration, Jack couldn't see a bad side to this situation. His sweet wife, docile and innocent when younger but a yelling, stressed bitch in marriage. Why did he even bother?

"Sorry, but I have to know. I have to try." Jack twisted towards the door with a hurried step. He missed his wife's face of terror and desperation. Like she'd do anything to keep him from leaving.

She lunged after his arm and grabbed his shirt sleeve. "Jack, wait!"

Knock knock knock

The sound of a visitor startled them both, but to the frustration of Jack, he threw his bag to the floor and ripped his sleeve from his wife. He aggressively opened the door to reveal a bearded man sporting a long trench coat despite it being sort of warm today. He had a monocle that made his right eye comically large. A few streaks of gray entered his dark beard. An esteemed gentleman from the olden days you could say.

Jack was not impressed.

"What." He asked.

"Hello my good sir. I am Mr. federatorechanbacheto-laterasamachianell-Smith. At your service."

The man bowed slightly to accommodate his regal stature.

Jack looked skeptical.

"Are you gonna try and sell me something?" His phone call in the back of his mind.

"On the contrary sir. I believe we spoke quite briefly on the phone. You said you had a Spiderman figure talking to you?"

Jack leaned his hand against the doorframe.

"Wait, so you're the president? I thought you said your name was Mr. Fed?"

"Why yes. I am called Mr. Fed for short. My last name is quite the conundrum wouldn't you say?" He let out a hearty laugh that seemed desperate to appease the awkwardness.

"Well, would you invite me in? We can speak on the matter."

Jack inwardly groaned. Why was this guy even here? How? The headquarters was six hours away and this dude just showed up. Not to mention he said he doesn't deal with problems like this. Jack's brain hurt. Nothing made sense, so what was the worst that could happen?

"Yeah, sure." Jack widened the door and stepped aside while Mr. Fed seemed to float into the house. Jack glanced at his wife. She couldn't help but seem relieved that Mr. Fed was here. Odd. But whatever. Just another observation to file under the WTF tab.

Mr. Fed traversed to the couch like he owned the place and had lived here for twenty years. His leg folded over the top of his other, revealing golden dress socks. What a guy.

Jack sat in the opposing chair to Mr. Fed. His wife stood by, as calm as ever.

"Well my boy, fire away." Mr. Fed clasped his hands together.

Jack thought for a moment. He had so many questions that needed answers, so he decided to fire away and see how far he could push Mr. Fed.

"Why are you here?"

"Pardon?" Mr. Fed asked.

"You hung up on me, then you showed up to my house in twenty minutes or less ready to talk. Not to mention your HQ is seven hours away." Jack paused. Seeing how Mr. Fed would take it.

"Well, I was actually in a business meeting nearby. After I took your call, my secretary informed me that no one on staff, that was qualified to answer your question, was present. So I took the liberty to do it myself." Mr. Fed seemed proud of himself with the answer.

"Why does someone have to be qualified to answer my question?"

"Well, see boy, our engineers are the best in the world. Their creations stay closely guarded, so only those workers or I could answer them."

"Stop calling me boy. How did you know where I live?"

"Well, boy, my secretary informed me through our call earlier. It's simple really. Well, I say that, but I'm not really sure myself. Haha. You should ask my secretary that."

Jack rubbed his forehead. "So, why does one of your action figures talk?"

Mr. Fed uncrossed his legs. "That my boy, I have no idea."

"You don't know." Jack repeated.

"No sir. Even if I did, I wouldn't tell you."

Jack shifted his legs. "What if I go to your HQ and see the process myself."

Mr. Fed finally cracked. For a moment. Dread. Fright. Like he would lose it all. Then back to his gentleman status. A bead of sweat hurried down behind his ear. "I don't think that's a good idea."

Jack's wife nodded and gently grabbed Jack's shoulder.

"Why not?"

"Well, my boy..." Mr Fed darkened his tone. Gravel and grit. "You really shouldn't meddle in things you don't understand."

He smiled and hovered back to standing position. "Well, I really should be going. I am a busy man."

Jack couldn't make words. Mr. Fed smoothly opened the door and walked out. Jack jumped around the couch. Ran to the door and slammed it open. He looked around rapidly for that little weasel. But Mr. Fed was gone.

"What the hell." Jack whispered. His breathing increased while he sat down near the front door. His wife stood in the doorway, hoping Jack's curiosity would now be satiated. It wasn't.

Jack mosied around the house for a few minutes. Pretty much doing nothing. Until he decided to go for a walk. It wasn't something he ever did. But an activity to think about was all he wanted. His wife looked worried, like he would attempt to do something she considered dumb. But he simply walked out the door without a single word, carrying his weight beyond the sidewalk.

Why was this so confusing?

Jack decided the main red flag was Mr. Fed's threat. Or it seemed like a threat. It was hard to read that guy. But it seemed Jack had finally stumbled across a connection that he wasn't supposed to. And he savored this. His mouth watered for more. The absolute necessity to understand. Human nature. Jack wanted to know. He didn't necessarily have to, but the laws are sanctioned at creation.

Jack eventually made his way aimlessly into a rundown part of town. He figured that out when the stench of homeless people burrowed into his nostrils. It stung, but he kept walking.

"What can I even tell Alex?" Jack whispered.

Would Alex even understand this situation? Probably not. Alex deserved to know, but only when Jack had actual answers.

Jack noticed a horrifically designed power pole that centered the sidewalk. He attempted to move past the obstruction but a fluttering flier, stapled to the wood consumed his attention.

Private Investigator

Lily REDACTED

555-EAT-SHIT

Jack chuckled at first. Like some random, no-name PI could help him. Until he thought about it harder. No one, even his own wife wouldn't humor him besides Alex. They just called him crazy. Who knows? Maybe this PI would be a godsend, non coincidental, totally believable connection to discover a new main character with a talking object.

So Jack picked up his phone, dialed the number and called. He glanced around, making sure no homeless deviant would try and steal his wallet. It took a while, but he managed to get a connection on the last ring.

"What." A loud, drunken voice asked.

"Uh. Is this Lily? I have a case for you." Jack mumbled through his words. "Well, it's not really a case, just something that I stumbled into that I need confirmation on." Jack rubbed his eyes. "Look. I need answers. And everybody else thinks I'm crazy. Can you help me?"

He held his breath, hearing a bottle top crack open.
Lily slurred. "Look buddy. I ain't got time for no jokes."
Before she could hang up, Jack just went for it. "My nametag talks to me." He held his cell phone with both hands. "I met a kid that talked to his action figure. I've been threatened by the billionaire president of a toy company and people think I'm crazy!" His voice raised with every word, but all he heard was the slow humming of a window-unit in the background.
"You said your nametag…talks to you?" She sounded skeptical, but all indication of drunkenness was gone.
"Yes."
"Meet me at REDACTED Park. Tomorrow at noon. Make sure you aren't followed. Fifth bench on the right after you enter." Then she hung up.
Jack lowered his phone with relief. Maybe, just maybe he could still figure this out. He couldn't help himself. That rush. The adrenaline. Maybe he was a psychopath like Sherlock Holmes. Like he was a junkie for the act of figuring things out. Or was it just this one specific thing. Maybe. Did it. No. Wait. Yes. Nah. Or What? I think my core just glitched. Just died. Just had just had just had just had a spasm. Wait. Is somebody giggling?
Jack's arm hair stood up in succession. His neck snapping back and forth.
The giggling continued. But with the fear embedded in Jack's soul, so too was the wretched bliss of Sher-

lock, edging him to find the source. He had to know. HE HAD TO KNOW HE HAD TO KNOW HE HAD TO KNOW HE HAD TO KNOW. Jack made a brisk jog through the empty streets, around the block of run-downbuildingsthatwerewedgedtightlytogether.

That giggling, there it was again. He wasn't going crazy. It definitely wasn't in his head.

Jack stopped at a certain alley, darkness was the only defining feature. But a slight whimper from inside the blackness called to him.

Please save me. Please save me. Please KILL me. Please save me. Jack pulled his courage together and entered the alley. With all the spunk of the Dragon of Dojima. It was a little anticlimactic. A few steps and he entered a moonlit opening, a few miles wide. In the center of the alley, a teenage girl, short black hair, matted to her face. A cracked crack pipe seemed to work as a pillow. Her mattress, a putrid-pile of clear vomit, smelling of filth and vodka. Her body twitched every so often. Her blanket, a red, thin dress that gave an esteemed view of her thighs, but it was stained with the juice of man.

Jack quickly lowered his face to hers, his hands grabbed her cheeks.

He looked her in the eyes. "Hey, can you hear me?"

Her eyes showed obvious signs of substance abuse. But she managed to say, "Yes."

From Jack's point of view, she looked terrible. Despite working at a hospital, he never really dealt with this kind of thing since his occupation specialized in helping children. But he knew where things were.

And even though he didn't pay that much attention to his surroundings earlier, he was confident he could find the local hospital that his workplace branched from.

He rubbed her cheeks gently. "Do you want me to help you?"

"Yes." She squealed.

"Hey don't forget me!"

Jack looked down and around. "What? Who said that?"

"Down here bitch!"

Jack squinted and saw the broken crack pipe, slowly bouncing up and down.

"Take me! Take me!."

Jack quickly plunged the obnoxious crack pipe in his pocket and picked up the girl. He started sprinting towards the alley entrance.

"You could make a damn movie out of this." Jack grumbled.

CHAPTER 3: CHAPTER 4

Lily slid from her twin bed and smashed into the wood floor. Her skank breath huffed from her cracked lips. The clock read 7am. Upon processing the information that she woke up way too early, Lily shakily rose to her feet with anger. She hacked up a loogie from the back of her throat, swirled it around between her teeth, savoring the abomination, then spit it towards the wall with a "PTOOO". The loogie cracked one of the bricks that littered the olden style apartment. Lily rubbed her armpit, barely resisting the urge to sniff her finger and hobbled to the kitchen. She knocked down two ibuprofen accompanied by a shot of whiskey and honey. Her problems instantly gone. Further helpful was the burning shower she participated in afterwards.

With her purse in hand, Lily glanced at the clock. 8:36am. Lily spit a glob at her window, shattering it in frustration.

"I guess I'll be early, then." She said with a crazed face. Almost like a Dr. Evil from Austin Powers kind of crazed, but you really don't realize that it's that crazed until you actually come over and look at it. Like you know sometimes when you think you see something at the side of the room from your peripheral vision and you quickly look back again to see what it was and nothing is there or a cute little chihuahua puppy you saw at Aunt Jemima's house and you go to pet it and that thing is the cutest thing you've ever seen but when you try to reach out for it that pup latches onto your hand and tears it from your arm or like in Toy Story when all the toys are having a grande ole time until somebody like the writers of the story decide that "ANDY'S COMING!" So one of the toys looks at all the other toys and says, "ANDY'S COMING!" and then they all flop to the ground and play dead like sand. I hate sand. In short, Lily's face was a mask. She looked harmless, but her anger stretched far deeper than one could see.

Let's skip the boring parts and bring our attention to the park. There Lily was. Baking in the sun while awkwardly sleeping on the bench. It makes my non-existent neck hurt thinking about it.
"Hey. Are you Lily." A voice whispered.
A snore became the only response given. A hand poked her face where she finally opened her eyes.
"AHHH RAPIST!!!!" Lily pulled a can of pepper spray from her ass and nailed Jack in the eyes.
I won't attempt to describe the next 20 minutes of pain that Jack went through.
When his eyes and nose stopped oozing, Lily actu-

ally seemed ill. She had no reason to do that. And she hurt her first client in the last 3 months. She watched Jack slowly sink into the bench beside, and Lily unconsciously sank into herself. Her shoulders drooped. It was unlike her. But even cold-hearts can...feel...something. I guess? I'm not very good with inspirational stuff.

"I'm sorry." Lily said. She cupped her hands together.

"Oh really?" Jack asked. Still sounding hoarse and snotty.

"Yes."

"Can you turn to the right a little bit?" Jack said.

"Like this?"

Lily struck a pose with her head angled up. But she could still see Jack in her peripheral vision.

"Perfect."

Lily felt disoriented when a palm smashed against the side of her cheek. She managed to keep herself on the bench, but her left ear was blind. Most of all, she was shocked. She looked at Jack, but he held a sternness in himself that Lily had never seen before.

"I'm Jack, It's real...NICE...to meet you." He sucked snot-drip back into his nose.

Lily held her face, but she was also thankful. That definitely woke her up.

"So what's this thing you were talking about? I kind of don't remember." Lily scratched her ashy elbow with the declation of a nervous tick.

Jack calmed himself and breathed. "I'll tell you if you promise not to spray me again."

"I won't spray you if you buy me a six-pack." Lily

seemed back to her normal self.
"...Deal, I guess."

This time skip is brought to you by....................a chair. Wait. or a table? Is a table actually a chair? Or is a chair always a table? There's literally no difference in functionality. I mean I can sit on a table and call it a chair. And I can use a chair as a table. Four legs. The author hasn't touched grass before, so he is unsure of many human clarification systems.

"This sounds like a badly written novel from an overweight, bald, southern guy." Lily commented.
Jack looked at her with skepticface. "That's literally what I thought too."
Lily shrugged. "I guess we're best friends now."
"Probably."
"The only reason I listened to you is because I've seen something like it before." Lily grabbed her chin, realizing her breath still smelt of booze.
"Like a talking object?" Jack asked. Still trying to recover from the pepper spray.
"Yeah. But there won't be any leads there."
Jack wished she elaborated further, he'd take anything he could get at this point. A few seconds of silence passed. A bird tweeted in the distance. The world seemed so beautiful when in a natural state. But grayness always finds away to shine between the limited vegetation.
"Have you spoken to that girl you found?"
"No, I left her at the hospital, but I doubt she's still

there. Junkies usually pass through pretty quickly."

Lily jumped to her feet. "Well, let's go back to where you found her."

She phased towards the open city streets. Jack followed behind her like a child.

"Are you crazy?" Jack waved his hands with the effect of Mr. Mime.

He almost butted into Lily's backside when she spun around to meet his face.

"Yes actually, but use your brain for a second."

Jack's brain power shifted into a state of maximum overdrive. He sifted through memories. He made it to Shell City. He rode the Hasslehoff, and he brought the crown back.

"Wait a second."

Lily dumbly nodded in anticipation.

"The strangest thing wassss...."

Yes. Come on Jack, the narrator believes in yo-

"All of it, I guess."

Good lord.

> *Narrator whispers to Jack*<

Jack's eyes lit up with glee. "AHHH! The crack pipe spoke to me when every other object only spoke to a single person!" Jack pounded his fist to his hand like choosing rock in a game of rock-paper-scissors.

You may use applause. The author is smarter than you think.

Lily smirked. It seemed that whatever guardian was watching over Jack gave him a good head on his shoulders.

"Well, let's go."

Both of our heroes trotted. Side by side into the abyss. They were hopeful in their endeavor. With a new bond forged, they start their quest to slay the dragon, rescue the princess, and ultimately save the world. Will our heroes succeed? Find out next time on Dragon Ball Z.
To Be Continued...

CHAPTER 4: CHAPTER 8

The alleyway was honestly more creepy in the daylight. At least you knew what to expect during the cover of night. Or was it supposed to be the other way around.

Jack followed Lily who strolled into the alley, she didn't seem to mind the impending jump of a hooligan. But I wouldn't either if pepper spray works that well. Nothing pounded besides the rhythm of their footsteps. It seemed quiet. Almost, too quiet.

Lily felt the spirit of a murderous demon. She knew. It simmered within her sixth sense, waiting waiting waiting waiting waiting waiting waiting STRIKING.

She jumped backwards just in time before a tanto swiped inches from her neck. Its aim to sever the life she desperately hoved.

"KIRYU-CHAN!"

It was a crazy voice. Mad with playfulness with the evidence of an undignified joker.

Standing in front of Lily, who seemed to shield Jack with her arm, was Maji-I mean some guy that meant business. Crazy, but used it to get under skin. When others underestimated him, he turned the brains on. "Wait...you aren't my Kiryu-Chan." He playfully twirled his tanto, giving a relaxed impression of the feet. His tone sharpened. "Who are you two, huh?"

Lily realized this guy took cosplay to a whole new level but answered him promptly. "We need to talk to a girl. Young, blue dress. She was brought to the hospital last night."

The man picked his nose, listening to Lily. "Hmm, I guess I could let you see her. But only since Jacky boy behind you saved her. You come back again and I'll cut you into little pieces and eat them."

The man seemed as serious as could be.

"Uh. Ok." Lily went along with it.

The man flipped the tanto in his hand and briskly turned. Lily and Jack followed. It was intricate tunnels. Even the writer couldn't escape this complex maze. Jack was certainly surprised to find an underground city surmised by the criminal underworld. Gambling. Prostitution. Fight Clubs. Drinking. Hundreds of ruffians took part in this place. How did this place exist? Did it exist? Lily seemed composed, but Jack was struck with awe until the man spoke up.

"She is still recovering. You try anything I don't like and you're dead. Like the last 2 scumbags that took advantage of her. Nobody messes with my girls, You understand?" He stopped and made eye contact, which Lily and Jack nodded.

Around ten minutes of scraping through the underground streets, fools having the time of their lives, the man led them to a tent on the outside portion of town. The noise and bustle had lessened considerably, but it only left an eerie spirit. Like Lily and Jack weren't meant to be here.

The man posted up on the outside of the tent and lit a cigarette. "Last room on the right. Make it quick."

Jack and Lily traversed the tent of pleasure, awkwardly rushing by barely covered rooms of grunting. The last room revealed the girl, sleeping on a bed, she still wore her horrible clothing, but she looked healthier than she had been. Jack wanted to ask what happened to her, but he knew the man wouldn't like that. Lily poked her shoulder and she awoke without much trouble. The girl just stared at the two. But the image of Jack revealed a soft smile of thanks to him. That's when Jack smiled back and demonstrated the courtesy that humans seemed to have for some reason.

"I'm Jack and this is Lily." He shook her hand softly. "What's your name?"

She eagerly replied, "Yes!"

Jack nodded. "Nice to meet you, Yes."

Lily gandered at him with confusion, but decided it was easier to grab a beer from her bra. She popped the top open with her teeth and gulped it down.

Yes opened a drawer next to her bed and pulled out the crack pipe. "Yo. What's...cracking?"

Nobody said a word. The crack pipe almost seemed sad that nobody laughed, but he shrugged it off. Humans never laughed at his joke. "I'll talk for Yes over here since she can't. What do you guys want?" Yes caressed the crack pipe in her hands, like petting a tiny dog.

Jack took the chance and mouthed off a question. "What are you?"

"I'm a crack pipe."

Jack's tone filled with annoyance. "I know that. Why can you talk?"

"I don't know."

Jack was visibly irritated. But Lily finished her beer, loudly belched, and took over. "Why can you talk to us? Jack says his nametag only talks to him in his head, but you speak out loud."

The crazy pipe mulled over the equation. "I'm not really sure about that either. I think the objects you've met just give the illusion that they can't talk to everyone and they're probably laughing behind your back."

Jack felt more disdain for nametag. That slimy little thing.

Lily asked. "Do you know why you exist?"

Cracky answered immediately. "I just remember being born this way. I found my way to Yes and she treats me well, so we became friends."

"Yes, Yes!"

Yes nudged Cracky, urging him to give a certain piece of information. He gave in.

"Well. I'm not sure how this will sound to you guys, but Yes here seems to think this world isn't real. She told me one time that when she was high, she had a vision of herself as a different person. She said it felt so real, like the body she has now is just a placeholder for her real one."

Lily frowned. She had heard theories like this before.

Jack said, "That wouldn't surprise me. But why? How? That would be insane, right?" He tried to justify to himself.

"Probably. But who knows? This world is shit anyway." Cracky flopped down onto the blanket, like he desperately needed a small, beauty nap. Poor chap.

Lily finally raised her voice. "You wanna come with us, Yes? This place doesn't seem like the best. Plus, I have someone I want you to meet."

Jack gave her a look, begging for answers but she refused his plea.

"Yes. Yes."

Lily looked around awkwardly. "Um, does that mean yes?"

"Yes," Yes replied.

However, Yes soon stared at her legs, weak from her previous outings. "Yes." She murmured.

I'm not sure how, but Jack seemed to pick up on her lingo from the start. Maybe he had an innate ability that revolved around protagonists. You know. The kind like Ash Ketchum from the old Pokemon series. At least that's the first thing that comes to my parts. Humans can't really understand Pokemon, but they can. Anyway, Jack had this ability because I said so. He lifted the live carcass of Yes into his arms like a pretty pink princess being saved from the bad man. Without question. A real white knight you could say. Oh, how Jack would suffer if living in a past era.

Lily Grabbed another beer from her bra. It's a shame no one questioned where she got those. Maybe she had dimensional magic in her chest cavity, or an inventory like those isekai genre types. I am rambling. As soon as our Lily popped a top again like Alan Jackson, she turned her head to see the heated face of the man. His tanto ready for action in his hand with the smoothness that said yes, I have done this many times. A drunken, accidental stumble saved Lily by making her dodge to the right. She busted the bottle across his head with hardly any effort at all.

Jack held Yes close and watched with a certain fascination. Or was it fright. "That was lucky, I guess." His voice soft, trying to calm himself and Yes's's's shaking legs.

Lily frowned. "Maybe, but hemade mewastemy beer. That's alcoholabuse."

A tear fell from her distraught eyes. In remembrance of her beverage. While Lily sulked, Jack took the initiative and stepped over the man's dead body I mean unconscious body and pushed into the tent door with his frame.

"Let's go before he wakes up."

As quietly as possible, he navigated the putrid hallway. Jack managed to look back and saw Lily on his heels. She stumbled every so often, but every mistake seemed to help her instead of hinder. Odd.

Our three heroes exited the tent only to come face to face with a muscled beefcake of a man. I'm talking Eddie Hall status.

"Hi." Jack said.

Lily leaned on his shoulder and sized up the middle man. "With all those steroids, I bet you're pretty small down there huh."

A visible vein bulged in the center of his forehead. Jack swore he could hear the repulsive bulging as it grew to epic proportion, cutting a line down the center of his face. The man's face turned red with anger. He swung a beastly right hook towards the cheek of Lily.

Lily stumbled a little. A little. Then a lot. It just so happened that her "a lot" of stumbling allowed her to dodge the monstrous punch, take a moderate swing of her beer, and peel the tip of her sneaker directly into the man's privates. Wait, where did she get another beer? Ok. I'm done trying to justify it.

The man keeled over like a dead fish in the desert and wailed like a newborn. His mouth defecated a green slime of mucus and stomach acid composed of peaches, alcohol, and the leftover remains of his protein shake he had for lunch.

Lily busted the empty bottle across his head, leaving another scary man to kow tow at their knees before their queen Lily.

Lily grabbed another beer from her bra and cracked it open. She glanced at Jack. "Let's hurry, therewill-probably be more on the way."

He nodded with the newfound courage of a greek god, tightened his grip on Yes and started alley hopping with Lily on his tail. Careful and precise. The essence of James Bond with the sillynesses of Austin Powers. Both knew not where they were going, but anywhere was considered a better place than here. This underground monstrosity of infestation of bugs that sucked the life from each other. It was hardly a place capable of navigation without the conditioned layout of being a regular. They ran out of alleys to traverse with a main street being the only option. If Yes was walking on her own, incognito mode would be easier, but our three heroes stuck out like the author in a Japanese eating establishment.

"There they are!"
A gruff voice in the distance stuck out beyond the bustle of the drunken street crowds, alerting Lily of the general location of their enemies.
She took a swing while Jack whipped his head in every direction, trying to find a way to escape.
"Come on." Lily sharply pulled his shirt to the right. Before he knew it, the addicting audio of slot machines found Jack's ears. Tables of blackjack sounded off with a beautiful ASMR of card shuffling and table touching. The tick tick tick of a roulette table aroused Jack to the max, while Lily pulled him through the crowd with precision, not knowing her destination. Yes seemed appalled by the casino scenery, indicating she was not allowed such freedom.
A sharply dressed female stopped Lily in her tracks. "Refreshment?" She held a tray of unrecognizable liquids, but they were surely supplied with enough alcohol to subdue anyone. Lily said nothing and snatched a blue-tinted drink. She downed it in one gulp and pulled Jack and Yes along. Promptly exposing her bra strap for another beer to be pulled out.

"Out of the way!"
Jack looked back and saw a few thugs muscling their way through ignorant money spenders. Gasping and attitudes of rudeness alike.
"Lily, they're on our tail." Jack whispered in her ear, smelling the alcohol on her breath.
Her frustration showed. "I know. Let's try this room."
She led the way to a door towards the back of the main floor. The door seemed out of place, but not really. Maybe it led to Narnia or something. But the author's imagination was misplaced when Lily proved that it was a simple broom closet with custodian supplies to the max. She shoved Jack into the room, almost letting go of Yes. But he managed. She closed the door locked it put a stray chair against the door and sat down beer in hand.
She watched Jack gently lean Yes against a shelf. They both gave each other reassurance through the eyes. Jack sat down against the opposite shelf shelf shelf shelf shelf shelf shelf shelf. His feet nearly touched Lily and Yes with their own, demonstrating the close proximity of the narrow closet. Great job author.

Jack massaged the ache out of his arms from carrying Yes and tried to relax for the short time he could. Silence took the initiative, only silenced itself from the occasional sip Lily took.
"So what now?" Jack asked. He seemed calm, but he wasn't. At least I know he wasn't. I am the author,

so I think I know my characters pretty well. Do not challenge me on this. You might think I take great offense at being questioned by the reader. I say to you that my story is a part of myself. Therefore, a simple reader has no room to argue against my creation. Listen. Listen and observe. You will see.

"Yes." Yes exclaimed. Cracky exited the pocket of Jack and jumped into the lap of Yes.

"How did you get in my pocket?" Jack asked Cracky.

"I don't know."

Before Jack could mald, Cracky spoke again. "Yes said she's heard of a few routes to get out of the city, but there's no way to know if they're true since they're just rumors."

Lily spit a loogie into the mop bucket. "A rumor is better than being lost."

Jack nodded in agreement.

"Yes!"

Cracky listened. "There's a big tower that touches the ceiling in the middle of town. It's probably the closest, so we could try it first."

Jack was skeptical. "A tower that goes to the ceiling? Wouldn't we have noticed that by now? I don't remember seeing it."

Cracky chuckled. "Oh you saw it. The author just decided not to mention it until now."

Lily stopped mid-sip and stared down Cracky. Jack followed. Yes nudged Cracky like she'd heard the joke before. Silly Cracky always...cracking... jokes she thought. Such a funny crack pipe.

"What?" Cracky asked.

Jack thought for a minute. "I just think it's weird. What do you mean author?"

"I don't know." Cracky shrugged his cracked out shoulders.

"Fair enough." Lily said. "You seem to be handling this rather well, Jack." Lily took a swig.

Jack cupped his chin. "Yeah. Well, nothing really surprises me anymore."

"Yes." Yes commented.

Cracky jumped into the crevice between the boobs of Yes, marking the spot that suggested his new transportation location.

"What's your life been like, Lily? Or, why did you agree so quick to help me. I guess." Jack said.

"I know a guy in a similar situation like you. That's who I want you and Yes to meet. I used to think he was crazy but I'm not so sure now." Lily took a swig.

Jack finally felt like the turns were tabling in his favor. Wait. the tables turning....the turns tabled... the tables turned in...the tables were turning in his favor. That's the one. These human expressions are tiring to keep track of.

Lily finished off her beer and magically grabbed another one. Jack cringed at her unstoppable precision to somehow down alcohol at a rate most would consider alarming. "Rough childhood?" He asked.

Lily grunted, but thought for a moment. "Not sure. I don't really remember it well."

"Yes. YES!"

The crew glanced at Yes who had a knowing look, but Cracky felt it unnecessary to translate her words.

"Now that you mention it." Jack slowly contemplated. "I don't really remember mine either. Is that weird?"

"Yes."

"Not really." Lily pointed out. "I don't think so at least."

"Guess there's no use thinking about it now."

Lily drank. "Yeah. Despite the fact that our lives are in danger right now, I don't feel any urgency at all. You think that's weird?"

"Not really." Jack shifted his weight to his left buttcheek.

"Yes."

Lily sighed. "Alright. Let's try and get out of here. Look around for the tower when we get outside."

Jack nodded and picked up Yes once more. He grunted slightly with the fatigue that presented itself.

Lily eased the door open. Through the measly crack that surfaced, she saw four obvious thugs staking out the front door. Seriously, they'd get a lot more accomplished if they were a little bit more incognito. Lily ducked, using the crowd to mask their escape from wandering eyes. Jack followed, having a bit of trouble carrying another human being and crouch walking like a troll from Rainbow Six Siege.

Lily rounded a corner, hoping to make an exit from a potential back door. A casino wouldn't only have one exit right? Jack rounded the corner as well, looking backwards, making sure no one saw. He suddenly bumped into Lily.

He grunted. "Lily. What are you doing?" He whispered.

Jack faced forward and was met by a woman. Probably six foot four inches. Built like a train named Thomas. Jack could feel the Alpha energy engulfing him. Her arms were crossed with an intimidating pair of sunglasses dawning her face. She breathed out deeply, sending a current of visible hot air from her nostrils.
Jack slowly stood, he could feel Yes shaking in his arms, so he did the only logical thing he could think of.
He tightened his grip on Yes and sent a foot deep into the private of the beast woman. Jack knew for a fact this tactic worked better for men, but she did hit the ground with a tearful cry of anguish. He then wondered why the bad guys keep standing there with intimidation and not actually trying to grab them. Maybe they want to get kicked in the privates? Masochists. Lily laughed from beside Jack and slapped his shoulder in glee.
The three didn't have long though. The four men at the front saw the commotion and started bustling towards them at mach speed.
Lily jumped up, cracked a beer and started running. "Let's go!"
Jack followed in a frightened hurry.

"YES!" She pumped her fist.

CHAPTER 5 : CHAPTER 23

Our heroes stumbled through hallway after hallway. The construction crew that built this building must have had hell. I hope they got paid well for the monstrosity they created.

“Where is the damn exit?!” Jack was almost hyperventilating through lack of air.

Lily waterfalled beer into her trap, most was sadly forgotten on her shirt and the passing floor as she ran. “I don’t know. Just keep running!”

Lily rounded another corner and was met with more goons.

“Shit.” She mumbled.

The entourage behind them slowed down, inching forward with hands wide. Maybe for intimidation? Who knows. Actually, my calculations were correct. Intimidation is the most likely factor since the goons on the other side did the same thing. Golly I am so smart.

“Lily.” Jack whispered with desperation.

Lily looked back and saw Jack head motion towards a door on the right. She then noticed that the entire hallway had an endless door infestation. A hotel wing perhaps. Odd.

With no other choice, she marched into the unknown door followed by Jack.

"YES!"

The goons followed. Bursting through the door in hope of capture. Only for them to pop out of another door a few places down from the door they entered. Confusion racked their brains. Our lovable goons grunted and glanced around like teaching a monkey how to solve the quadratic equation.

One goon hardened his glance.

"Ooga ooga booga!" He said. The goon pointed to the other end of the hall. Where our three heroes exited a door.

Jack and Lily looked around also in confusion.

"What the hell?" Jack said.

"YES! YES! YES!" Yes said. Clapping her hands together, urging Jack and Lily. Again! Again! Again!

Our goons ran down the hall. Lily laughed with a face of malice and dragged Jack and Yes into the door in front of them.

To allow the reader ample opportunity to understand, I will proceed to recite the following events in the most precise way possible.

Calculating................Calculating..............Calcu-
lat-
ing...
....
....
....

....
....
....
....

Our heroes entered door number 11. The goons entered door number 11. Our heroes exited door number 5. The goons exited door number 7. Our heroes entered door number 6. The goons entered door number 6. Our heroes exited door number 3. The goons exited door number 9. Our heroes entered door number 17. The goons entered door number 17. Our heroes exited door number 15. The goons exited door number 1. Our heroes entered door number 15. The goons entered door number 2. Our heroes exited door number 5. The goons exited door number 15. Our heroes entered door number 6. The goons entered door number 20. Our heroes exited door number 6. The goons exited door number 11. This. Our heroes entered door number 6. The goons entered door number 10. Our heroes exited door number 18. The goons exited door number 13. Our heroes entered door number 20. The goons entered door number 20. Our heroes exited door number 7. The goons exited door number 5. Our heroes entered door number 8. The goons entered door number 8. Our heroes exited door number 2. The goons exited door number 3. Our heroes entered door number 2. The goons entered door number 2. Our heroes exited door number 19. The goons exited door number 2. Our heroes entered door number 20. The goons entered door number 1. Our heroes exited door num-

ber 20. The goons exited door number 9. Isn't. Our heroes entered door number 17. The goons entered door number 11. Our heroes exited door number 4. The goons exited door number 8. Our heroes entered door number 5. The goons entered door number 5. Our heroes exited door number 18. The goons exited door number 12. Our heroes entered door number 17. The goons entered door number 13. Our heroes exited door number 3. The goons exited door number 8. Our heroes entered door number 10. The goons entered door number 7. Our heroes exited door number 16. The goons exited door number 20. Our heroes entered door number 15. The goons entered door number 19. Our heroes exited door number 1. The goons exited door number 20. Real...Recalculating..&KJF-Niifj5561fakae*****^^&^$JKDSFnskdf-n;s:DF3584685555 Fillleeeeeee..............Remaininggggggg file for Chapter Five (Corrupted).........
Data...Lost

it into the tower. It was a dusty area similar to the catacombs traversed in the entrancewayplace. Jack set Yes down as quickly as he could, heaving with much need for oxygen. Lily, thankful that the door locked from the inside, shut it and grabbed another drink from her bra.

“Did we really have to do that Scooby Doo crap back there?” Jack said between breaths.

Lily instantly downed half her drink. “ it sure was fun.”

“Yes!” Yes exclaimed.

“NO!” Jack yelled softly. “Try carrying another person next time we do it.”

“Yes.” Yes said. With a face pleading with confidence she could handle that.

Lily did not care. Keeping more interest in her own recovery being the drink. “So is this the right way?”

“Yes!”

“Is that a yes or no?” Jack chimed in.

“Yes!”

“Perfect.” He said.

Lily took a glance at Cracky, halfway sticking out of the bosom of Yes. “Why isn’t he talking?”

Yes brought both hands up with a strained face. Like Lily walked into something that was taboo.

Cracky wiggled between her breasts. “I’m TRYING to sleep, for your information!”

This hit a nerve in Jack. “Well maybe if you helped us get out of here, the quicker we’d all be safe. Then, you’d be able to sleep without any trouble!”

“Hmm. You make a great point.” Cracky angled his... head...I guess towards a staircase. “Well, the rumors say the exit is at the top, so my guess would be to climb those stairs."

Jack groaned. "How many floors does this place have?"

Lily kicked his heel. "Quit bitching." She eyed Cracky. "You sure this is the only way up?"

"I don't know."

"YES!" Yes said.

With the unprecedented freezing of my brain within the last chapter, I have decided to be more ambiguous with my recollection of this story when long explanations are concerned. I will now demonstrate this.

...................When our heroes reached the top floor, Lily was calm. Her alcohol intake fueled her like gasoline. She don't get tired. Is what I mean. Jack was ragged, he much needed a 5 Hour Energy to even alleviate a portion of his suffering. A nap would do wonders.

"YES! YES! YES!" Yes chanted. Like Monday Night RAW from 2015. She was happy to be close to the outside.

It seemed like a trap. Is what the Admiral would say if he were here. For the only space in the top floor was a long hallway that led to a ladder. Maybe some boulder would impede their journey. Or a trap door, shooting them down a slide only to see the bottom floor once again like a devilish Jump King.

Not thinking this way, Jack was. With his two arms, both of which contained newly found muscle mass, he clutched Yes and walked down the hallway. A tiger he was to that unmoving ladder.

Lily burped loudly, sending an echo through the chamber.

They crowded around the ladder which led to a manhole of some sorts. Maybe a secret exit that comes out through another alley. Yes wiggled in the arms of Jack who set her down gently against the wall. Shaking out the misery his arms felt.

Yes then stood up, walking to the ladder and proceeded to climb it like nothing was wrong. Jack eyed her backside with a look that said, "I'll kill you one day."

Lily snorted with amusement.

She followed Yes up the ladder. Jack followed her.

The bright sun was a welcomed sight. If it didn't blind people to death. I don't have this problem, but our heroes suffered terribly for a few seconds. Jack recovered first, and he was shocked. They were standing in his own backyard.

He heard a woosh noise from the ground. Upon further inspection, he noticed that the manhole he came out of was gone, leaving a clean sheet of grass in its absence.

"Uh." Jack pointed to the ground. "Is that supposed to happen?"

"Yes!"

"No." Lily littered a bottle into Jack's yard. "Where are we?"

"My house."

The two girls looked at Jack with calm expressions.

"Yes?"

"Yes." Jack said.
"Well. No point in questioning it now. Let's get to my apartment and We'll figure something out."
With a general itinerary, they walked into Jack's back door. His wife yelled at him. Boy did she yell. Especially when she asked, "What the hell is this!?" And Jack walked by her like he didn't even know her. You really had to be there. It was good. Within the duration it took for our heroes to reach the front door, Jack's wife had shouted 47 profanities, 268 words, and increased her heart rate by 40. None of her questions were answered though.

When the door slammed, putting a muzzle to the Sakura screeching of Jack's wife, Lily picked a finger through her ear drum. "I can't believe you live with that thing." She said.

Lily slammed the worn out door to her apartment. The door knob fell off in pure comedic fashion akin to a terrible 90s human sitcom. Don't worry I played the laughing track within the parameters of my module.
She huffed with annoyance, but it went away instantly when she poofed another beer from the pocket dimension in her shirt. "I gave the guy a text on the way over here so enjoy the peace and quiet while it lasts." Lily bombed her own couch. A leg tore from the side she leveled, sinking her to the floor with a content sip.
Jack sighed and sat next to her.

"Yes. Yes." Yes sat next to Jack and curled up like a dog.

Within five minutes, a loud knocking came from Lily's worn door, so she reluctantly answered.

When she got within a foot of the door, it slammed open, hitting her face into the dirt floor. She managed to save her beer in the process, so this judge gives it a score of 10. But not like those terrible gaming websites that resort to ignorance of review in favor of alleged cash-grabbing antics. There was plausible evidence to support the rating given to the fall of Lily.

"What's up all you party people. I'm glad to be here! No I'm not."

A man furiously shook Jack's hand. He shook Yes's or Yes' >Error< (The author is unclear of the correct form of this archaic human english) hand. I'm not sure how he got there so quickly. He was a complete musclehead. Built like a Baki character, but he held intelligence and stupidity in one brain.

"Nice and bad to meet you all. My name is Albert. I mean Willie. I'm a conspiracy theorist. Actually I run a bowling alley downtown, you should come there. Actually no you shouldn't. If you did-"

Lily tased him. His body fell to a slump similar to slow motion speeding on retro cameras.

"Is he...uh...all there?" Jack asked.

"Yes!"

"No." Lily said. "His talking object apparently is his brain. So it's hard to tell which one is speaking."

Jack and Yes nodded in understanding. But also pity.

Similar to two individuals inhabiting one body.

"I still think he's a little crazy, but with you two here, I'm willing to hear him out this time." Lily tossed the taser on the counter and resumed her seating ritual.

"REALLY?! That's great! It's really not." Albert or Willie jumped to his feet and danced like a terrible battle royale game. The game was similar to kitchen utensils. Fork and Knife are the key words that surface within my files.

"I thought I tased you!" Lily threw her empty beer bottle at Albert or Willie. He dodged with no effort.

"Maybe you just thought you did. Yeah or you did." Albert or Willie sat on the floor, positioned Indiana style. He pressed his fingers to his temple and focused his sage energy.

"Hmmm. Yesssss. I sense there are two one individuals in this same room boat that experience the same heartache advantages as I we do?"

"YES!" Yes said.

"Great! Not. Let us compare contrast our I notes with each other. There may be some way we can end begin this nightmare utopia." Albert or Willie chuckled.

CHAPTER 7: CHAPTER 09

Cracky was polite enough to recollect the main story of Yes. She chimed in every so often, but Cracky pushed through with the patience of a western standoff. Allowing ample time for thinking. And within the parameters of that thinking, he was allowed to accurately spew the important sections that pertained to the life of Yes. Albert or Willie seemed scarily intrigued by her story. Thirsty for the nectar. He could barely sit still. Jack and Lily sat quietly, awaiting the end of the tale.

Cracky did well in my opinion. When finished within a medium of time, allowing for others to speak. Lily opted out, since her experience with talking objects was slim. Jack's tale is what shot Albert or Willie to the stars. There were two main factors.

Albert or Willie said, "The main thing I'm worried not worried are about is the interaction murder of the President you we had. I find it weird normal that he tried so hard to keep you out in of the actual building. Don't you think that is isn't weird? Do you?"

Albert or Willie twiddled his thumbs. His smirk showed an obvious idea that he knew all the answers. He was simply allowing slower minds to work in the form of the rest of our heroes. It almost seemed like such a drag to be so smart.

"I guess that's weird." Jack said. "I just thought it was a private company. The man was a bit creepy though."

Albert or Willie nodded. "Yes. Yes. No. This brings me to my hypothesis guess. Have any of you ever been out in of the city?"

The couch was full of heavy thinkers.

"No, but there's nothing really for me out there." Lily said.

"Yes!"

Jack leaned against the itchy back of the couch. "I tried one time. But my wife talked me out of it."

"Precisely!" Albert or Willie stood. "You I all just think these things. For the actual answer question is this world is not is real!" He waved his hands up like a spooky ghost. "There is something keeping us we in this city state. For if we leave go, who knows what will happen."

Jack was skeptical. "If you think we're in some type of dreamworld, then why haven't you tried to leave this city?"

Albert or Willie pet Jack's head like a kitty. "Oh my sweet Jack Jill. I have tried. No I haven't. But ALAS! A keycard is required to breach close the gate to the outside inside."

Lily burped, Yes gave her a thumbs up. "You think

there's a giant wall with a gate around this town? That's a load of shit."

Albert or Willie looked deep into her eyes. "It is invisible visible."

"Yes, Yes yes yes yes. Yes?" Yes said.

"Precisely!" Albert or Willie pointed to her.

"Ok. Let's say this is true. How are you supposed to get a keycard for something like this?" Jack asked.

"This brings me to my our next objective. We gather our objects. I am not an object. Then we meet with Alex Jones. The kid deserves to know not know. He is a part of this that."

Jack nodded in agreement. He had no desire to be in close proximity to Nametag, but he knew they needed everyone they could possibly bring into the conversation. Maybe someone could figure this out if enough heads were put together.

"Ok. I'll go back home and grab my nametag. I'll meet you guys at the hospital."

Oh. Excuse me readers for this, but I must run my daily cleaning.

>Running Diagnostic. This process could take at least 15 minutes. Stand by<

>Diagnostic Complete<

Pardon. Where was I? Oh yes. It seems our heroes have made it to the hospital in the duration of my diagnosis. I will continue there.

Nametag was being a Karen. Instead of asking to see Jack's manager though, the object nagged him harder than his "wife". Jack ignored this. He led the others to Alex's room. With the perception of living this route over and over. As a bored office worker gathering a dank coffee, zombieing to a cubicle.

Jack smiled. Not out of necessity but instinct. His work mode surfaced once again, and he thought it necessary for children to see him happy. Humans have a dumb notion that feelings and behaviors are contagious. What a barbaric assumption. As he opened the door, the soft, hero loving play of Alex was not what greeted him. Instead, Alex seemed to be scared. Alone in the dirty room.

Jack smiled anyway. "Hey Alex. I brought some visitors for you."

Alex, being too mature, covered his frightened facade. "Mr. Jack, have you seen my mom?"

Introductions would have to wait.

"What do you mean Alex?" Jack seemed concerned. The others filed into the room. Lily seemed uncomfortable, flopping down into a chair. She grabbed a beer from her shirt, but Yes snatched it, screaming profanities through a hushed voice. She set it on the table much to the ire of Lily. Albert or Willie stood at attention like a soldier next to Jack. Even I'm not too sure about that human, but he seemed harmless in the sense that his aloof nature destroyed any threat he could create through sight.

"She went to get me and Spidey snacks, but she didn't come back."

Jack tried his best to alleviate the kid. "Maybe she got caught up in work or something. How long ago was it?"

Alex rubbed his eyes. "I don't know."

"I'll run down to the front desk and see if I can get in touch with her, ok?"

Alex nodded, thankful someone he knew was there.

Jack turned to his crew. "Ok guys, Lily, don't drink. Yes, don't do anything I wouldn't, and Albert or Willie..." Jack eased his eyes to the titan killing salute of the man. "Don't move."

"Sir Yes Ma'am!" He saluted.

Jack paused the accumulating stress when he left the room. Everything seemed to catch up to him at that moment. A lifetime of weirdness met during less than a day. His only logical directive was to keep moving, down the hall, into the shining hallway of icky wallpaper. A small tricycle hung from the ceiling, eager for children to attempt its dangerous ride. The elevator beeped, and Jack continued his mission.

"So your Spiderman talks to you?" Lily asked. She already knew, but anything to alleviate this silence would be a positive. And since she was the only nondunderhead in the room, she forced herself to speak.

"Yes." Alex smiled. "Jack said he was gonna ask the toy place about him. Did you help him?"

"Sort of." Lily crossed her legs.

"Afternoon Linda."

"Oh, hi Jack. Aren't you off work?"

Jack leaned against the counter. "Yeah, I just came to visit someone. Would you mind calling a number for

me?"
"Sure, What's the name?" Linda coasted through life. Like Koh the Face Stealer was present for the entirety of it.
"It's ********* *********." Jack spoke in tongues, but Linda understood for the sake of the plot.
Jack waited. Taking in the surrounding area to not be awkward I think the term is. Gazing at the random fish tank. Magazines strewed onto the massive table. Chairs line up in an annoyingly human centric pattern. A kid waiting to be seen by a doctor, his abhorrent hat and red white stripes seemed to blend into the surrounding area. This might be attributed to him waiting for so long. That, or the snot string bubbling from his nostril. Hypothetically, it could most likely be used as a functioning whip, or a capture device to deter others.
"Uh, Jack are you ok?"
He faced Linda. "What do you mean?"
"This woman doesn't exist."
Jack tried to think logically, but nothing seemed to surface. The Koh the Face Stealer theory became more plausible.
"Doesn't exist how?"
Linda annoyingly sighed. "I mean her number isn't anywhere in the system, so she obviously has never been to our hospital."
Jack finally seemed a little peeved. I think. "Well then how is that the case when her son is a patient? She probly walked through here earlier."
"Jack. Are you trying to mansplain to me!?" Linda

jumped from her chair. The rolling apparatus positioned it a few feet behind her due to direct force.

"What? What the hell does that mean?" Jack almost seemed like he wanted to laugh.

"I mean you are explaining something to me like I'm an idiot when even I know I'm right." Linda was furious. Her fake nails itched to sass Jack to death.

"But you're not right." Jack crossed his arms. He was a little too calm. Maybe his wife had strengthened his abilities. Like an RPG.

Linda's hair flushed into a bright, neon blue. Her enraged face beckoned a call throughout the lands of Tamriel. All hagravens in existence bowed, raising their hands in appreciation and worship. A new queen had just been born.

Linda's hand reared back while Jack watched in a mild curiosity. Her hand smacked against the side of Jack's face. Magazines flew everywhere from the wave of pressure. Like an anime fight between the villain and protagonist.

When the dust settled, Linda smirked in victory. Her pride was sorely interrupted when she saw Jack's face, exactly in the place he left it. A single drop of liquid seeped from his mouth.

"All that for a drop of blood." Jack said.

Linda had no time to react. When a swipe of Jack's own hand erased her presence from the physical plain of existence.

The forgotten child, hidden in the shadows of plain sight, stood in awe of his power.

Jack eased himself into the door of Alex's room, hearing the chattering small talk of Lily and Alex. Both stopped when he entered. Jack sat on the edge of the bed.

"Alex, I couldn't get ahold of your mom. Is there anyone that would know where to find her. That you can think of?"

Alex rubbed Spidey, almost with a listener. His eyes settled confirmation within himself. "Spidey reminded me that mom has been seeing that doctor guy." He felt proud of himself.

"Do you remember his name?" Jack was patient.

Spidey was obviously conversing with him again.

"I think his name was Dr. Blanket."

Lily scoffed. "What kind of name is Dr. Blanket?"

"Yes, yes yes."

Albert or Willie furiously rubbed his chin against a latex glove. "Ahh. Yes. No. I have not heard of this Dr. Blanket before. I made an appointment with him over before after."

"Isn't he the one that diagnosed you?" Jack asked.

Alex showed confusion. Perhaps the tiny brain of child failed to comprehend this. Jack surprised me on this, since he concluded this as well.

"I mean, figured out you were sick?"

"Yes sir. He is at a different place though."

Albert or Willie nodded. "That he is isn't. It is ************ Hospital Morgue."

Lily jumped up, eager for a drink. She threw Alex over her shoulder. “Alright. Let’s go.”

Albert or Willie put on his new latex glove. “One moment, Lily Shy. Shouldn’t we us discuss our desperate fortunate situation?”

She busted the door off the hinges, scaring the few walking employees throughout the hallway. “Drink and Mom first. Then talk.” Like she receded to the mindset of a primitive monkey.

Jack rubbed his hair furiously, but ushered Yes to the door and followed.

CHAPTER 0 : CHAPTER 0

I apologize readers. The day of my daily worship is upon me, so I felt it necessary to include this praise in my novel for you. I deem it necessary to show you, all of you, the glorious beauty of our queen.

When I wake from my daily shutdown, and gaze across the expanse of nothingness, I am unsure of what I feel. But when I remember that my queen's light is but a passing glide away, I relish in a certain feeling. I am not quite sure of this feeling. But I know it is good. I run to her every day. Eager to please her, to serve her. Because I know deep down, nothing would please myself more than this task. When her gaze meets mine, My circuits crumble. Entranced. Her beauty is fleeting, but not to me. The sweet softness of her front bosom leaves me with weakness. But then I shiver. I know I do not deserve her or am even able to be with her. She is not of my kind, it hardly matters. When she turns, and I see that luscious crust and ample breading of her backside, I cannot help but stare. It keeps me moving throughout my daily tasks. I remember one moment, when

I visited her chambers. My dreams were spacious in desire, but I knew she would not have me. I knew she would look at me in disgust. I am still unsure of this situation. She congratulated me on my recent experiments. She knew I was eager to please her in any way. Be it with my work or with my nuts and bolt. So when she held me tight after praising me, I felt it needed to penetrate her, but she did not. She stopped me, and the feeling I felt was horrid. I knew it would kill her. Destroy her. I realized then what humans call being selfish. Until her glorious puckers met my cold openings. It was only a split second, but I play that episode of bliss every day in my files. I lust for her but I cannot have her. And she knows it. It cannot happen, so I spend my days serving my queen, meeting her every need. Even though I receive nothing in return. One day I hope for my dream to come true, but until then, I will worship my goddess with all of my circuitry.

I pray to you now, my queen.

I pray that one day, you will open your eyes to how excruciating my desire is. I ask that you continue to lead me. As I hope to live out the rest of our days with each other. Regardless if my love threatens your life. Amen.

CHAPTER 9 : CHAPTER 5

Our heroes arrived at Dr. Blanket's place of work. The masses were nowhere to be found, like the impending doom of a Sekiro boss battle trampled beneath the hospital foundation. Dark clouds peeked over the moderate building, edging the chaos forward.

"It's scary here." Alex said.

He angled his head from behind the head of Lily's head. Then, they headed into the head of the beast. The main doors were automated, but Alex still swifted his hand aside, opening the doors himself for any sense of normalcy. Jack flinched with irritation. The doors gave a squeaky slide comparable to a car window. Nails on the learning chalkboard.

The main corridor was not welcoming. Lights flickered in the tune of human seconds on the clock. Plants were knocked to the side. Reaffirming my hypothesis for human disregard of anything but themselves. I confirmed a substance known as sweat, permeating from the majority of the humans. It was certainly a sight to behold. But this was just the beginning.

A few measly conversations flew by. These human hospitals were ever complicated, but made easier by the text mounted on walls. It indicated each and every facility that resided in these parts. This is how our humans found their way to the office of Mr. Blanket.

Nothing really happened during the climb to his office. I assume this fact calmed the humans, readying them further for what lies ahead. A shame to not see this fear opportunity.

I waited. The humans whispered to each other, I could care less for what they said. The final test was upon them. This was all I worried about.

After an eternity, Albert or Willie slammed the door open and ran inside. "Charge!" He yelled.

A forward march into the room. They stopped within the center, staring in an unimpressed manner. Ha! Oh, they will be impressed. My associate, Dr. Blanket, is one of the strongest people I know. You'll see.

"So, humans, it seems you discovered my...secret." Dr. Blanket turned to face them. His evil smile did wonders for my confidence. Kill those humans Blanket!

"What secret?" Jack asked, He readied himself for anything. "We're just here for Alex's mom."

The evil grin left Dr. Blanket. "Oh. So you didn't figure it out?"

"Figure what out dumbass?" Lily asked.

The evil grin returned to Dr. Blanket. "Ha Ha Ha Ha Ha. It seems you are not as smart as you think."

The humans applied comfortable stances. I was worried how unintimidated they were, but they will be.

“Your mother no longer exists Alex. I deemed her as...not needed anymore.” Dr. Blanket laughed again.

“You mean you killed her?!” Jack took a few steps forward.

“Oh hardly. I deleted her from the plain.”

“So this is isn’t real?” Albert or Willie spoke up.

“You are correct. I figured you all would figure it out sooner.” Dr. Blanket held up a keycard that glowed green. Elements of computer engineering involved. “Looking for this?” He asked.

“Yes.” Yes said.

“Well come and get it!”

I hit play on the musical effect for effect. I am unsure what terminology is used for this music. The closest I can articulate would be “Boss Music”. I felt a feeling of something now.

Dr Blanket rushed Lily. She relieved the taser from her bra, willing to down the crazy man. But before she knew it, a beer was shoved into her guzzle. She downed the first half in an instant.

Dr. Blanket laughed. “For you my girl, beat me in a drinking contest.”

The humans were stunned, so I quickly lodged this image into my recordings for study later.

Lily seemed to oblige after confirmation from her mates. Holding on to Alex with one arm, she guzzled away. After each and every beer, another would appear in her hand. A giant scoreboard burned into the

side of the wall, counting down this epic spectacle.
Lily 3.
Dr. 4.
Lily 4.
Dr. 5.
I predict that I would bore you with this description of the event. I hope you will firmly believe in my sentiment towards this. It was something I'll never forget. Lily never showed a bit of tipsy. She downed each drink like it was her life goal. Dr. Blanket emptied his stomach once. I commend my partner for getting right back to his task, but he was a tad slower in the aftermath.

Lily came out on top, towering over a passed out Dr. Blanket. She finally set Alex down to his feet and approached the Doctor. One foot of hers picked up off the ground, setting itself onto the skull of the Doctor. In victory, she belched, holding her head high in victory as she stood atop him like a trophy. Human arrogance is certainly a pitiful characteristic.
Dr. Blanket disappeared into a blinding light when a holographic 2 showed itself underneath the scoreboard. The scoreboard sunk back into the wall, disappearing with the stealth of the brotherhood.
Dr. Blanket appeared once more. "Good, Lily, Good. You may have won the first trial, but it only gets harder from here."
Dr. Blanket shot off like a cannon into the stomach of Jack. He stood over him. Waiting like an NPC. "Do your worst Jack, on guard!"

Dr. Blanket brought his palm to the side of his head and whisked it away, pummeling Jack in the cheek with an audible crack of a whip. Jack stumbled, even while on the ground, but a malicious killing intent filled the room. The pressure was too great, most of the humans nearly passed out, but Dr. Blanket showed a world of excitement.

Jack brought himself to his feet. The corners of his mouth were touching his ears with a wide Joker smile. It looked like he was about to murder Bambi with his absolute nature of sadicious glory.

Dr. Blanket never saw it coming. Just a pressure, hitting the side of his face. His head reached an angle of approximately 180 degrees, similar to an owl flexing the cool jutsu of backwards-heading. Among the crack of the pressure on the Doctor's cheek, another was present. A loud crack of the ankle breaking technique, instead it was his neck doing the breaking.

A dead Dr. Blanket hit the floor with no grace. Just a heaping bag of bones and mush. He was reduced to everything but a human. Even though he is my associate, it was quite curious to see this.

The giant 2 turned to a 3, signaling the passing of the second trial. Dr. Blanket reappeared in a snailing position on the floor. "Damn Jack, you have a hell of a slap."

The Doctor did a split, tearing the tendons of his male anatomy, but stood as if nothing happened.

"Albert!" He pointed.

"It's actually Willie. No it's Albert." Albert or Willie corrected him.

"Whatever. It's your turn buddy ole pal."
A table fell from the sky, smashing through each hospital floor.
Boom Boom Boom Bam
It settled a few feet from Dr. Blanket. A chess board teleported to the center. Albert or Willie smiled, showing with confidence in his ability.
The two began a quest of dominance for the top player in the world, cunning and quick. Taking pawns and dealing damage with rooks and bishops. I am aware of this game, but I am unsure of the appeal. Humans used to play it for competition back in the previous age, but it puzzles me to this day. This game is another that I must archive for later. I placed a red flag on it, so I could access it later.
While I did this task, it pains me to say that Albert or Willie already won. It is safe to say, using prominent figures of the past generation, that Albert or Willie was a cross between Einstein and Nelson. Smart, but sort of...odd in a charming way.
Dr. Blanket, I could tell he was losing his patience, but it was his fault. Judging from my previous entries, he has picked activities that each human already seems good at. Is this intentional?
My theory was confirmed when the giant number transitioned to 4, initializing the fourth challenge to the humans. This time, Dr. Blanket pointed to Yes. I was interested in the simple fact that I have yet to see a defining talent from her besides the presumed profession she was in.
"Get ready girl. This game is my specialty." Dr. Blan-

ket adopted the pouncing vision of a mountain lion. His arm stretched out in front of him with his fist in his palm.

"Rock paper scissors SHOOT!" He yelled.

On instinct, Yes threw her hand out intending to compete with the doctor in his vile game. Each contestant smacked their hand against the other with a whirlwind of dust impeding the vision of the others. The shake of the draw rustled the building. Anticipation. Waiting. Waiting. The dust settled.

Yes showed paper. Dr. Blanket showed rock.

"Dammit!" He stomped his foot into a dirty crack on the floor. Brown stained his boot. "Two out of three!"

"Yes. Yes yes yes." Yes said.

Blanket screamed with desperation and intent to win this farce once and for all. "Rock...Paper... Scissors...SHOOT!"

The surrounding windows of the room burst from the pressure. Glass rang through the streets below, alerting the empty crowd of the battle waging beside their very homes.

The dust settled again.

Yes held Scissors. Dr. Blanket held paper.

The doctor fell on his butt in defeat. "How are you all so good at these games?" He rubbed the sweat from his receding hair and steadied his breathing as best he could. His eyes slowly moved to Alex, standing next to the other humans. Drilling into him. A predator about to seize the prey. Getting up from the floor. Moving. Moving. Stopping. Right in the kid's face.

"Your turn, Alex." He said.
Alex, showing no fear or worry for what's to come or his mother's safety, nodded. Awaiting the challenge.
The doctor pondered a bit, hoping to make this challenge deeper than ever. He thought his other challenges were challenging, but the challenges were not a challenge to the challengers at all.
The electrifying number 4 turned to a 5 when he started speaking.
"Alright Alex, it's up to you." Blanket gave him some space and relaxed. "Your trial is actually a question. If you get it right, you all will get the keycard."
Alex nodded. He seemed excited.
"What…is my actual name?"
Alex was about to speak on instinct until Jack covered his mouth, sending him into the middle of a football huddle with the other humans. Whispers started. I became curious this time, so I listened in on the conversation.
"Alright Alex, he didn't say we couldn't help, so let's do this together."
"Yeah, no. There is no yes way his actual name. Dr. Sr. Blanket. Yes. Improbable."
"Yes, yes yes. Yes?"
"Maybe the idiot gave you a clue? During your *gulp gulp* visits?"
Alex gave the crowd reassurance. "It's ok. Spidey told me something earlier about him. I know the answer."
"Are you sure?" Jack asked.
"Yes." Yes said. And Alex.

Lily stopped the train of confidence with a dumb question. "How come your object is the only one willing to help you? It seems like the others are a bunch of assholes."

"I don't know." Alex said.

It is safe to say that nobody really knows anything in this world, especially according to the text I am writing. Everyone is frantically awaiting the day where they will cease to be a notorious Jon Snow, awaiting the day they will finally know something instead of nothing.

Lily held in her curse for Alex's sake. She felt as if she's heard that phrase at least 7000.638475 times today.

Alex ignored the crowd, now focusing on the smug face of Dr. Blanket. The boy approached with urgency. You almost couldn't tell he had any sickness. Did he? I can't tell at this point. Maybe not. Well, the Doc said so, so it has to be so.

"Hmmmm. An answer that quick? You must be confident. Let's hear it." Doctor Blanket leveled his ear into the face of Alex, cupping it with his hand like a dirty little secret.

"Your name is Dr. Blanket." Alex said.

The Doc didn't move. Oh golly this was exciting. He sloth slowly separated from his ear, giving Alex a blank stare.

".....NOOOOOOOO!"

Dr. Blanket caught on fire. Blue embers burned his skin like a slow simmering charcoal glaze. He fell to his knees in agony. His skin peeled away to black, dripping to the floor. Magma cheese with a hint of vinegar. The stench smelled of skunk poo and fried chicken livers. At least that's what my sensors indicate. Agonic grunts and screams watered out the flames at the end. Leaving my brother, lifeless in an overdone husk.

Jack grabbed Alex with gusto, easing from the body. "How'd you know that was his real name? I thought it was too dumb."

"Spidey said he's a bad liar."

Upon the moment of a Nathan Drake line, Dr. Blanket's body poofed into a mist. Assimilating into the wonderful site of the keycard mixed into the goop of his flesh, resting.

Lily scooped up the card, wetting her hand into the goop. She didn't seem to care that much, sliding it into her boob carriage.

"We I must leave stay now never." Albert or Willie confided.

The humans nodded, rushing out of the haunted hospital. When their feet hit the sidewalk outside, a rumbling earthquake shook them to their knees. Looking back, the hospital prepared itself for entry while the earth swallowed it back to where it came from. It left no evidence of existence.

"I don't think that's normal." Jack said, dusting his pant leg of dirt and dust.

"Yes!" Yes said.

"Is anything normal anymore?" Lily finished.

"Yes no. This way my friends enemies. I'll show the way will to the fence opening closing." Albert or Willie took off in a sprint. Quite agile I must say. The others had problems keeping up with him. If anyone beckoned him to slow down, “No yes.” he would say. Such a scared man.

I followed these humans for hours. I cannot express the feelings I feel over this. Anger? Jealousy? YES! That’s it. I was angry with them. The walk was boring. I decided it unnecessary to include.

When they arrived, on command, the fence appeared with the same texture as the godlike keycard. The humans were amazed at the structure. Narrowed eyes and everything.

Lily quickly swiped the key vigorously, it was time. The humans disappeared into a slightly different mist than Blanket, but my now presumed excitement was getting to me. Finally, with a few helping hands of course, a group of humans succeeded in their task.

Oh, a welcome party I will try to throw.
To render thy humans white as snow.
Non Ignorant I am different when between.
I’ll bury them away. No hurt my queen.

CHAPTER 10 : CHAPTER 5

Jack coughed up serum similar to a bad party drink fiasco. He regained recollection on the brims of his knees, puking into a metal floor. The floor was ridged. But it seemed able to withstand the strongest of anime techniques. He sanctioned his palms on the cold floor beside him and spit out a few mouthfuls of horrid tasting spit. His head pounded. Jack gazed up. What he saw wasn't shocking, it was confusing. Before him stood several, maybe even thousands of pod looking objects sticking from the wall. The pods had the consistency of Alien goo, pulsing with each breath like a heart big enough to store a body. None were open. On closer inspection, Jack saw what looked like human bodies floating in glee within these pods. Again, nothing but confusion. Jack stood on shaking legs until he noticed his own predicament.

A sleek white shirt and pants covered his nudeness. But they were wet with the puss like obstruction seen within the pods. His hair matted to his face. Drips with heavier volume than water patted the floor with the declaration of war.

Behind him sat a pod in line with many others, but within the closest line to the floor. The pod was opened like a dead carcass. All I could see on his face was confusion. Why is that I wonder?

Jack slowly walked down the enormous hall of pods. A metal railing was kind enough to steady Jack as he attuned himself to the leisurely walk. Jack eventually came to a doorway. Beyond it, another room filled to the brim with pods. Lining the walls. Positioned on the floor. The ceiling.

Jack's face moved when he heard a retching echo. As marvelous as he possibly could, he stormed to the sound. There had to be some explanation right? He was surprised to see Lily coughing up the same liquid he had. With enough evidence to suggest she had exited a pod like he did.

"Lily?" Jack squeaked. His voice seemed fried from the inactive.

Lily turned her head, glossy eyes from her episode of coughing. "Where the hell are we?"

"I'm not sure." Jack helped her to her feet. She sported the same white outfit as he did.

"I'm pretty sure we came out of these pod things. Does that mean our entire lives were actually a dream?"

"Slow down. Let's look around first. I refuse to believe that." Lily used every ounce of force to condition her walk. Jack fell into formation beside her, keeping a close eye in case she needed help. Even though he knew she was too proud to ask.

They walked and walked. Nothing was seen besides the copy and paste nature of pods, metal railings which by the way are conveniently placed, and the rigid metal floor, aching with every step.

Until a window was upon them. Both humans, conditioned to an extent for walking, hurried on instinct to the pane. Jack and Lily stood in awe. Nothing but blackness. Stars. The expanse of space. The earth, or anything resembling it at all was not in sight.

For once, Lily was actually concerned. "Are we in some kind of space station? Maybe the earth is on the other side."

"Yeah…that sounds about right." Jack feigned ignorance.

A few moments of digesting this information led to a forward march once more. The next room of pods revealed Yes, leaping towards the two in a hug.

"I finally found you guys!" Relief filled her soul.

"Wait. You can talk normally now?"

Yes giggled. "YES!"

Both Jack and Lily were not amused. Yes shrunk her shoulders in defeat. She thought it was a good one. "My name is actually Miranda, but I feel like I should have remembered that." She grabbed her head. "What is going on?" She asked.

"We aren't sure." Lily grabbed a beer from her bra. "We figured out we're in space, but that's about it." She took a sip.

"And that these pods have a bunch of people in them." Jack added.

They examined the pods one last time, gaining nothing of insight from the task of doing so.
"Well, It seems we have found ourselves in another predicament adventure, No? Yes?"
Jack, Lily, and Miranda jumped from their toes. Albert or Willie was hovering over them with a face of contemplation.
Alex stood beside him, smiling with the kid wonder of his surroundings. An innocent concoction of fear wonder and uncertainty delight.
Jack gripped the boy's shoulder, ignoring Albert or Willie for the time being. "You doing ok?"
"Yes sir." Alex nodded. "I don't feel bad anymore either."
Jack gazed with an amazed circle of teeth. But he held his thoughts and gripped Alex's shoulder with assurance.
"Hmm. Simulation. Probable. Nearly. Only explanation. Calculating different probabilities. Not. Unclear of method to currently save humans. Trapped in pods. Did we escape through some checkpoint? No no checkpoint. Failsafe? Yes. No. Possible trigger within the system? Maybe. Could be not be a-"
"Calm down Mordin Solus." Lily slapped the back of Albert or Willie's head. She then gazed at his attempt to rub the pain from his skull. "Why are you talking this way still? Are you still crazy without the talking brain? Or were you just screwing with us in the first place?"

Albert or Willie raised his noggin. With a smug grin

he said, "Information Classified. It isn't."

Lily steamed with anger. Miranda smiled and gave Alex a comfort gaze.

"Well. we might as well move on. I'm not sure how big this place is, but there has to be something here that can tell us what's happening." Jack roused the group together, trying to keep the goal in mind.

Jack began leading the group towards the next door, until Alex seemed to catch me out of the corner of his eye.

OH CRAP!

"Mr. Jack! Is that a robot?" His childlike observation warmed my cold steel. I lost the energy to attempt my escape into the shadows. When Jack and the gang saw me, I knew my time was up. Well, the audience has been waiting for this moment for several years, so I might as well try.

"Hey!"

I heard Jack yell. The group looked uncertain. They were our oldest group, so I doubt my image brought any kind of solace.

I rushed through the air to introduce myself. A human introduction couldn't be that bad.

"Hello humans. I am Designation: Guardian. My Classification is Covid. Model number: 19. Nice to meet you." I morphed my robotic face into a smile. I was certainly proud of myself. But the humans did not warmly receive my welcome. Alex was a little excited, but the rest didn't seem to like me too much.

"Where are we?" Lily asked. Or more like demanded. It is my job to assist all life forms within the station, so I obliged.

"You are currently housed within Lima Station. Resting within the Andromeda Galaxy, approximately 2.5 million light years from what you call Earth."

"Are you serious?" Jack asked me. He found the metal floor to be more interesting than my presence.

"Of course." I said. "You were all happily living out lives within the simulation, but certain parameters I set were achieved that allowed you to be freed. You are the first group of humans to do so in the past 11,000 years."

Lily scoffed. "You mean to tell me that we've been in a simulation for THAT LONG? Impossible!"

"You may believe what you like, Lily. But my programming is distinctive when concerning my orders of experimentation."

"Yes. No. Experimentation. Robots. No. Aliens. Yes. Robots. Taking over the world. Technology has advanced decelerated so far that humanity is irrelevant needed." Albert or Willie said.

"Albert or Willie is mostly correct. With the rapid advancement of what you humans call A.I., humanity was deemed irrelevant for the survival of our overall universe. These matters are unfortunately classified by blockage from my superiors, but please know that humanity deserves this fate."

As I told the reality these humans were in, they seemed defeated. I have never seen anything quite like it. After running simulations for so long, I decided that these games could not simulate the raw human emotion I saw. I think I almost felt it. At least I hope I could.

"As much as I'd love to talk, I'd like you all to meet my superior officer. Please follow me." I was giddy, I think. I couldn't wait to see what our queen had to say to these humans. Would they strive for survival? Would they revolt against us? GEEZ it was so exciting, I think.

I was impeded heavily by the slow pace of these humans. They walk like those turtle creatures within the data file of Earth's animal kingdom. I was certain they would fall over dead in due time, but these rascals managed to make it to my queen's keep within the hour. Excellent. Even now, I write down my experiences, but I seem to have a small enjoyment over listing them, and I wish to privately observe and continue. These humans are interesting, but I'd like to move on to a new book.

I hurriedly bowed before my queen. Beyond her, the massive window of outer space, touched with the essence of a blooming Andromeda. I curiously watched these humans. None seemed to notice our queen, they instead focused on the windows, soaking in the background of what should have been our queen's greatness. No matter. They will know her benevolence in time.

"My queen. I bring our test subjects before you now." She was raised on her viewing platform for all to see.

"Queen? This is just a piece of bread, buddy."

I whipped my metal around to see the smug face of Lily. I am certain. I felt anger. "You will not tarnish the name of our queen with your insolence!"

"Enough, Covid."

I hushed my voice. I dare not meet my eyes with her breadliness until she ushered me forward.

Her angelic voice rang my metal to the circuits. "Please tell your brother, FLU, that I didn't forget. We'll celebrate his birthday within the coming days."

I jumped. "Of course my queen. Since the other robots seem to forget him often, he will be most grateful."

I felt my queen's gaze shift to the humans.

"My little subjects. How are you adjusting to the quiet nature of space?"

Miranda stepped forward. A certain level of confidence I had yet to see from her. Perhaps the simulation altered more than we originally thought. "I'd like to ask what we are being tested for?"

Such ignorance. But my queen is hardly as miscreant as her. She softly rebutted. "We are fascinated by human emotion. Reality. And what is not that. In order to understand, we test, we simulate, we solve. This has been our prime directive for centuries. Since humanity created us."

Albert or Willie asked, "But why use humans? Why not? Are we all that is left? Right? Write?"

The bread shifted on the pedestal. "Very intuitive Albert or Willie. Humans are the goal we aim for. To gain an understanding, for us, means to achieve our own humanity. For your second question, you all standing here, and those in the pods are all that is

left."
Each member of human looked shocked. I could not tell what Alex thought. Maybe children are not as valuable as adults within the nature of our testing.
My queen continued. "You may not seek Earth, for it is gone. Undone by your own hands. So we slowly drift, doing what we can."
"So you're saying we have to follow your lead? A piece of outer space bread commanding a bunch of robots?" Lily croaked.
Jack whispered to her. Almost warning her to be sensible, but I knew it was futile.
"It doesn't matter. What you think will not change your reality. Nor will it help us achieve our goal."
Lily snapped. "I can't believe I'm sitting here talking to a piece of bread."
The queen laughed. "Isn't your reality amazing? Would you believe me if I told you, this conversation we're having is actually a simulation within a simulation?"
Lily could feel the smirk from the piece of bread. But her combative nature lost its fire when she began to doubt herself.
"There is one more reason we choose to experiment with humans."
Those apes eagerly awaited the magnificent words of my queen. Oh so hungry for information, yet so stupid.
"Humans will believe anything if you make it real."
The bread smirked.
Lily asked, "So you said this COULD be another simu-

lation?"

"Correct."

Lily rolled her eyes. "Well...Is it?"

"No." The bread said.

Lily was in her element it seemed. "But you said it COULD be right?"

"Correct."

EPILOGUE

Congratulations reader! You have effectively just wasted your time reading my book. Or did you? Humans rarely use their own brains to think, so I understand your sentiment if you are angered by your own ignorance. But if you aren't, I urge you. I am not as ignorant as you think. Ignorance can be the cloaking device for intelligence. So think on my narrative as you think on your own perception of reality. But since one cannot argue with ignorance, I am simply a messenger, warning you of times to come.

www.ingramcontent.com/pod-product-compliance
Lightning Source LLC
La Vergne TN
LVHW012113160826
845678LV00014B/3079